Nora's hea...

She hadn't ... ... the grassy hill from the highway. She had heard nothing. They were just suddenly there behind her.

What if the kidnapper was in the backyard at Nightingale Hall?

Nora had already begun to turn, but she was stopped in mid-spin and lifted off her feet by something smooth and strong wrapped around her neck and tugged backward.

The only sound she had time to make was a strangled, gasped, "No!"

Terrifying thrillers by Diane Hoh:

Funhouse
The Accident
The Invitation
The Train
The Fever
Nightmare Hall: The Silent Scream
Nightmare Hall: The Roommate
Nightmare Hall: Deadly Attraction
Nightmare Hall: The Wish
Nightmare Hall: The Scream Team
Nightmare Hall: Guilty
Nightmare Hall: Pretty Please
Nightmare Hall: The Experiment
Nightmare Hall: The Night Walker
Nightmare Hall: Sorority Sister
Nightmare Hall: Last Date
Nightmare Hall: The Whisperer
Nightmare Hall: Monster
Nightmare Hall: The Initiation
Nightmare Hall: Truth or Die
Nightmare Hall: Book of Horrors
Nightmare Hall: Last Breath
Nightmare Hall: Win, Lose or Die
Nightmare Hall: The Coffin
Nightmare Hall: Deadly Visions
Nightmare Hall: Student Body
Nightmare Hall: The Vampire's Kiss
Nightmare Hall: Dark Moon
Nightmare Hall: The Biker
Nightmare Hall: Captives
Nightmare Hall: Revenge
Nightmare Hall: Kidnapped

NIGHTMARE HALL

Kidnapped

DIANE HOH

SCHOLASTIC INC.
New York Toronto London Auckland Sydney

ISBN 0-590-56867-1

12 11 10 9 8 7 6 5 4 3 2 1   5 6 7 8 9/9 0/0

Printed in the U.S.A.   01

First Scholastic printing, September 1995

Prologue

Dark.

Dark and dim and cold.

Not like home.

Home. So hard to remember.

Why haven't they come to get me? Don't they want me anymore? Was I bad?

I wasn't bad. They should come get me. I don't want to be here. I hate this place.

I hate them for not coming to find me.

If they don't come, I'll hate them more.

Forever.

If they don't come, I'll punish them.

I will.

Chapter 1

The second floor of Nightingale Hall smelled of lemon oil and lilac, and was very quiet. Nora Mulgrew could hear the slapping of her own, sneakered footsteps echoing behind her on the hardwood floor, as if someone were following her as she hurried along the dim, shadowed hallway.

No one was following her. There wasn't anyone in Nightingale Hall *to* follow her. Nora thought of this time period between the end of the summer sessions on campus and the beginning of the new fall term as "dead time" because nothing much was happening. The other residents of the huge, dark-red brick house high on a hill overlooking the highway between campus and the town of Twin Falls had returned to their hometowns or gone on vacation. Nora hadn't wanted to return to the cold, distant aunt who had raised her, and she couldn't afford a vacation. So she had stayed on at Nightingale Hall, alone in the huge three-story house except for the housemother, Isobel Coates, who came and went. On this sultry August morning, Mrs. Coates was in Twin Falls, running her Saturday errands.

Nora's coworkers at the campus day care center had stared at her when she told them where she was living, and had then been aghast when she'd added that she was temporarily the only resident of Nightingale Hall.

Mark Fitzhugh, "Fitz" to his friends, had stopped wiping the nose of a two-year-old to say, "You live *where?*"

Nora had only been on campus a week, enrolled in a summer class and working part-time in the center. She hadn't had time yet to hear any rumors about Nightingale Hall.

"They don't call that place Nightmare Hall for no reason," Fitz continued. He was tall and very thin, with curly, red hair and friendly blue eyes. Nora was impressed by how kind and patient he was with the children, even the older, brattier ones. "It's not just that it looks creepy. Some pretty scary things have gone on in there, including, rumor has it, a couple of deaths. I can't believe you're staying there alone. How come you didn't board on campus?

The dorms are pretty deserted right now. No problem getting a room."

"Nightingale Hall is cheaper. Besides, I like old houses. And I like my privacy. The house-mother leaves me alone. I can come and go as I please, and it's very quiet there."

"I've noticed that."

That confused Nora. "That it's quiet there?"

"No. That you like your privacy." Then a pair of four-year-old twins began squabbling over a piece of bubblegum, and Fitz ran to disentangle them.

What was wrong with liking your privacy? Didn't everyone?

Yes, of course they did, Nora told herself. They just don't carry it to extremes like you. That's what Fitz meant.

Although she liked the people she worked with and had gone to Vinnie's for pizza and Burgers, Etc., the long, silver diner up the road from campus, with them, had even gone to a party or two with Fitz and Sabra, Amy and Lucas, she had rebuffed efforts on their part to become more involved. She had to eat, after all. But she had no time for close friends or an active social life. She was busy with the summer class and her part-time work. If she became overstressed by adding a lot of social activities, she could find herself in bed with a migraine headache. Migraines were the worst kind of torture. She had to be careful not to overdo it, or she would have to pay.

"You don't know how to have fun," Amy Tarantino had accused, only half-joking.

But I do have fun, Nora had thought to herself. I have fun with the kids. They make me laugh. Especially Mindy.

Mindy Donner was an adorable three-year-old with blonde curls and huge brown eyes, the daughter of a history professor. Since her mother had been hospitalized with a serious illness, the child had become increasingly attached to Nora, and the feeling was definitely mutual.

"It isn't wise to become emotionally attached to the children," the center's director, Helen Kieffer had told Nora in a cool voice just before the summer session ended and Nora was about to go full-time at the center until fall classes began. "And certainly it isn't wise to favor one child. The other children have seen those stuffed, crocheted animals you've been giving her. She carries them around with her as if they're her lifeline. Giving her gifts could set her apart from the other children. You wouldn't want that, Nora. Mindy is especially vulnerable right now, with her mother ill, and you mustn't take advantage of that fact. Keep your distance, please."

Nora ignored the advice. Keep her distance? Ridiculous! Mindy, usually a bright, happy child, was suffering from her mother's absence, anyone could see that. She needed reassurance. If she chose to come to Nora for that, it would be cruel to reject her.

Still, she had made one concession to Helen's request. Now, whenever she unearthed from the still-unpacked trunk in her room another one of the crocheted animals her mother had made for her, she took it to Mindy's house and gave it to her there instead of at the center. Professor Donner didn't seem to mind. He seemed, in fact, grateful for the extra attention being given his small daughter.

The toy Nora had found this morning, when she was looking for a pair of khaki shorts, was a pink kangaroo, complete with a tiny, crocheted kangaroo baby in its pouch. Mindy would love it.

I loved it, Nora thought to herself as she hurried up Faculty Row. Taller than average and so thin she had trouble finding a watch that didn't slip and slide around on her wrist, Nora walked very fast even when she wasn't in a hurry, as if there were something waiting for her somewhere and if she dawdled, it would disappear before she got there. Her small, oval face was set in deep concentration, as it almost always was, and wispy tendrils of soft, pale hair escaped their neat, thick, French braid as she walked. Halfway up Faculty Row, she approached a white picket fence surrounding a small, pretty antique brick house. Her serious brown eyes scanned the well-groomed front yard for some sign of a little girl with blonde curls.

She wasn't there.

Nora opened the gate and hurried up the narrow walkway to the front stoop. Although it was only ten in the morning, the heat was already suffocating. She was glad she'd worn the khaki shorts and a white tank top instead of the jeans and T-shirt she'd planned on. But the heat and thick humidity worried her. She was more prone to migraines when the heat was intolerable. Should have taken an aspirin before I left the house, she scolded silently.

To take her mind off the headache worry, she focused her attention on the toy she was carrying in a plastic bag. The pink kangaroo had been her favorite when she was Mindy's age. Her mother had suggested she call it

"Roo" in honor of one of Winnie-the-Pooh's friends. Nora had answered matter-of-factly, "No. Somebody already *used* that name. I don't want no used name. I want a brand-new one." She had named the baby kangaroo "Bounce."

It was time now for another child to enjoy it. She'd have to tell Mindy not to take this one to the center, though. Helen might notice and then she'd know that Nora had disobeyed her. Might even fire her. Nora needed the job. Besides, she loved it. She didn't want to lose it.

"Is Mindy here?" she asked the housekeeper who answered the door. "I have something for her."

The woman, almost as tall and wide as the doorway, her bulk belted at the middle by a flowered apron tied around her waist, shook her head. An elaborate upswept hairdo, stiff with hairspray, remained obediently in place. "She's out back. Playing nice and quiet. Threw a tantrum when I told her it was Saturday and the center wasn't open. She sure does like that place." Thick, dark brown brows came together in disapproval. "In my day, children stayed home with their mothers, where they belong. But I don't say anything, not my business." She opened the screen door then to take a closer look at Nora. "You're Nora, aren't you?

The one Mindy's so crazy about."

"I'm crazy about her, too," Nora answered. Tiny little drums began pounding behind her ears. Oh, no. No. She hadn't had a headache since she'd arrived on campus. She'd been hoping they were gone forever. "Could I see her just for a minute? Maybe there's something you need to do. An errand or something? I could keep an eye on her for you."

Exactly the right thing to say. The woman's face brightened, and she gestured to Nora to step inside. "Well, now that you mention it, I just might run next door and talk to my friend Teresa for a minute or two. She's got a recipe I've been wanting to borrow. Chocolate soufflé. Might cheer the Professor up some. He's been pretty down in the dumps lately. I would never leave the child alone, not even for a second, but if you're with her, I guess it'd be all right."

"I won't leave until you come back, I promise," Nora assured her.

"Well, of course not. I'll only be a minute."

Mindy was delighted to see Nora, and thrilled with the new toy, which she promptly positioned on the white wicker porch swing, where the other animals were already gathered. "We're having breakfast," she told Nora, "but Maynard," pointing to an elephant with a large rip in his floppy left ear, "don't want to eat his muffin." There was, of course, no muffin. Mindy had a very active imagination, one of the many things Nora loved about her.

By the time Nora had persuaded Maynard to eat his "muffin," the stultifying heat had increased and Nora's head was pounding with what was unmistakably the birth of a migraine. Depressed, she told herself she should at least be grateful that it had attacked on a Saturday, when she didn't have to work. Helen didn't like absentee employees. There was too much work at the center for people to be calling in sick.

Where was Mary, the housekeeper? She had said she'd only be gone a few minutes. It was already close to half an hour.

If I don't get back to my room and lie down soon, Nora thought despairingly, I won't be able to get home at all. I'll have to ask someone to drive me. Humiliating. Utterly humiliating. But the migraines totally incapacitated her, to a point where the tiniest movement nauseated her. To find relief, she had to be lying flat on her back, completely still, in a totally quiet room. One of the major appeals of an empty, cemetery-silent off-campus dorm.

"Don't you feel good, Norrie?" Mindy asked

her, peering up into Nora's face. "Your face looks like your tummy hurts. Are you sick?" The anxiety in her voice came, Nora guessed, from her mother's hospitalization. She didn't want Nora ending up there, too.

"No, I'm not sick, honey." Having a headache wasn't really being sick. "But I need to go home. As soon as Mary comes back."

When Mindy began to argue and tease Nora to stay longer, "for all the day, Norrie, please?" Nora's head felt as if it were going to explode. And when a suddenly petulant Mindy whined repeatedly, "Don't go, Norrie, I got nobody to play with," the nasal, high-pitched sound disintegrated the last of Nora's patience.

"Stop whining!" she commanded, her own voice high-pitched, just as Mary came around a corner of the house. The woman's eyes widened in shock, and she hurried over to Mindy's side.

"I'm . . . I'm sorry," Nora stammered, putting a hand to her head. "It's just . . . I have a headache, and it's so hot. . . ."

The woman's level gaze was unrelenting. She might become annoyed and snap at the little girl herself occasionally, but she wasn't about to tolerate anyone else doing so. "You can leave now," she said flatly, her freckled arms on the child's shoulders, as if protecting her.

"Mindy, I . . ." Nora began, but the little girl, tears of hurt sparkling in her brown eyes, turned and buried her face in the housekeeper's apron. "I'll see you on Monday," Nora added helplessly. There was nothing left to do then but leave.

The ride back to Nightingale Hall on the small, yellow university shuttle bus was agonizing. Every bump sent shafts of pain throughout Nora's skull, as if very sharp knives were being driven into her eyes. Nausea overtook her and just when she thought she couldn't sit upright another second, the bus pulled to a stop at the bottom of the gravel driveway leading up to the house.

She walked gingerly, almost staggering as she made her way up the hill under the shadows of the huge, gnarled old oaks guarding the wide-porched structure. There was no breeze at all stirring the leaves to provide respite from the murderous heat.

Mrs. Coates hadn't returned home. Inside, the house was utterly quiet. It wasn't air-conditioned, but the thick brick walls and the heavy maroon draperies on the long, narrow windows kept the first floor cool.

The second floor was not so cool. The curtains were white lace, and provided no protection from the blazing sun outside. Nora's room was like an oven. She moved stiffly to the window to shut it, pulling down the shade in hopes of keeping the sun's heat as well as its light away. She needed unbroken darkness.

Then, still moving cautiously, one small step at a time so as not to jar her body unduly, she went across the hall to the bathroom, where she swallowed two aspirin and wet a washcloth at the sink.

Returning to her room, she closed the door and moved to the bed. Carefully, moving in slow motion, she lay down on top of the quilted spread and placed the cool washcloth over her eyes.

Then, she prayed for sleep.

When it finally came, she sank into it as if it were a cool, sparkling pool that would soothe her hot, dry skin and wash away the agonizing pain in her skull.

And was awakened sometime later by the sound of pounding. But . . . the handyman was away. Who would be pounding?

It wasn't the sound of the handyman fixing a loose shutter or a porch step. It was the sound of feet. Footsteps. Too heavy to belong to Mrs. Coates. Someone else's feet were pounding . . . up the stairs?

Nora raised herself up on one elbow. The room was dark, and cooler than it had been earlier. She blinked once, twice, checking . . . the headache was gone. Sometimes they lasted for hours, occasionally even more than one day. She'd been lucky this time. She had tended to it early. One more battle won. There would be others, but this one, she'd won.

Pounding again, but this time, the sound was different. Not footsteps now. A fist, hammering on her door. And then a male voice, deep, authoritative. "Ms. Mulgrew? You in there?"

Knocking, more insistent this time. The voice louder. "Ms. Mulgrew? You there? It's campus security, miss. We need to talk to you."

Nora's eyes opened fully. Security?

Fitz's words about Nightingale Hall came back to her. "Some pretty scary things have gone on in there." Had something new and terrible happened while she was sleeping?

"Ms. Mulgrew!"

Nora slid off the bed, and cautiously opened the door.

Two campus security officers, a man and a woman, both in brown uniforms, were standing in the hall beside an anxious-looking Mrs. Coates. "Nora," the woman said nervously, "these officers need to talk to you about that little Donner girl."

Nora looked at the officers inquiringly. "Mindy? What about her?"

The two officers exchanged a glance, then one said, "You saw her this morning? The Donner girl?"

Nora nodded. "Yes. I took her a toy. But I had a headache, so I didn't stay. Why?" Had something happened to Mindy's father? Nora's heart sank. It was bad enough that her mother was in the hospital. She needed her father now, more than ever. "Why?" Nora repeated. "What's going on?"

"Maybe we should talk inside," the male officer said, glancing around the hall.

"There's no one else in the house," Nora said impatiently. "Just tell me what's going *on*! Has something happened? Where is Mindy?"

"Well, that's what we'd like to know, miss," the female officer said. "I'm Joyce Adelphi, and this is Jerry Blount. It seems the little girl is missing."

Nora's body, relaxed from her nap, went rigid with shock. A gasp of disbelief escaped her lips. "Missing? Mindy? No . . ."

Then her shock was compounded as Officer Joyce Adelphi added, "The thing is, Miss, the housekeeper at the Donner place and some other people we've talked to seem to feel you might know where the little girl is."

Nora's mouth fell open. The words rang in her ears. She stared at the officer. "Excuse me?"

"Could we just come inside and discuss this, Miss?" Officer Blount asked, his voice impatient.

Nora knew she couldn't keep them out. She wanted to. She wanted to shut the door in their faces and go back to bed and back to sleep and wake up some other time to find that she had dreamed the whole thing. She would wake up and discover that it wasn't real, after all. No one had come pounding up the stairs, no one had knocked on her door, and she hadn't heard a police officer say to her, "It seems the little girl is missing."

And they thought *she* knew where Mindy was?

Nora opened the door wider, stood aside, and waved the trio into her room.

Forever after, her mind would fix that moment in time as the moment when her nightmare began.

Chapter 2

"I want to go home. I don't like this place. You said my daddy would be here, and he's not. You take me home now."

"We're not going home just yet. Your daddy's busy. He told me to take care of you."

"No, he didn't. I don't like you. I want Norrie."

"Nora. Her name is Nora. You're old enough to say it right."

"She don't care if I call her Norrie. You're not the boss of me."

"Yes, I am. For now, anyway. You go lie down on that bed and I'll tell you a story."

"A story? Good as what Norrie tells me? She tells the best stories."

"Better. Hush, now. Just be quiet and listen. I'll sit over here in this rocking chair, so you can see me the whole time and know you're not alone."

anything out. Not now. Now that I've started, I have to do it right.

"Sleep tight. Back as soon as I can. When I come back, I'll tell you some more of the story. But I can't tell you all of it. Because there isn't any ending just yet.

"But there will be. Soon. Very soon, that's a promise . . ."

The door opened, then closed, and a key turned in the lock.

The child with the golden curls slept on.

Chapter 3

"Could we have a little light in here?" Officer Adelphi asked Nora as they entered the room.

"I was sleeping. Migraine," Nora explained as she moved to the window to release the shade. She winced as the light flooded in.

"Sleeping?"

Nora turned back to face the officers and Mrs. Coates. "Yes. It's the only thing that works when a migraine hits." She clasped her hands together in front of her and leaned against the old wooden dresser. "Sometimes. Sometimes it works."

She remembered then why they were there. Mindy was missing? Why weren't they out looking for her? "Are you sure Mindy is missing?" she asked anxiously. "She must have wandered up the street to play with a friend."

"Anyone else in the house?"

Nora stared at the officers as Officer Adelphi moved to her closet to peer around inside, and Officer Blount took a position at the foot of the bed, a white notebook in his hands. She couldn't be sure which one of them had asked her the question. "Anyone else in what house?" she asked, confused.

The male officer, holding the notebook and a pencil, sighed. "This house," he said. "While you were . . . asleep. Anyone else here at the time?"

She stood up straighter. When she spoke, her voice was thick with confusion. "No. I'm the only one here right now. Why? I mean, why do you want to know that? Even if there had been someone else here, they wouldn't have known if I was sleeping or not, would they? Who would be nosy enough to open the door and look in my room?"

He shrugged. "Friends. Looking for you. Maybe wanting to go shopping at the mall or take a bike ride in the park or go for a boat ride on the river."

"I don't have time to do those things. I work full-time at the campus day care center." Nora almost added, "And I don't have many friends, either," but she stopped herself in time. Her social life wasn't any of his business. Or . . . she felt a sudden chill . . . *was* it? Wasn't he *making* it his business?

Who had told the police that Nora Mulgrew might know where Mindy Donner was? Why would someone say that?

Mary? Did she think Nora had come back and taken Mindy for a walk? But I would never do that without asking first, Nora thought.

But the officer had said, "The housekeeper and some other people . . ."

What other people?

"Could I answer your questions some other time?" Nora asked politely. "If Mindy really is missing, I'd like to go help look for her. I'm sure she's just in the neighborhood somewhere." Of course she was. Mindy couldn't *really* be missing.

"No, I'm afraid not, Ms. Mulgrew," Officer Adelphi said. "In fact, we were kind of hoping you'd take a ride up to campus with us so we could have a nice, quiet little talk."

Nora froze in place. Wait a sec here! What was happening! Were they serious?

Her eyes, filled with deepening confusion, and a hint of panic, moved to the elderly housemother's kind face. "Mrs. Coates?"

The woman shook her head sadly. "I'm

sorry, dear, but if these officers want you to go with them, I suppose you should go. It's the only way to straighten things out."

Nora couldn't give in that quickly or easily. The only thing that seemed important just then was finding Mindy. How could she help do that if she was sitting in an office on campus talking to security officers? "Mrs. Coates, you know I have migraines! I told you about it when I first arrived. *Tell* these people!"

Mrs. Coates cleared her throat. "Well, yes dear," she said uncertainly, "you did say that, of course. But . . . you haven't had any up until now, so I don't know . . ." Her voice trailed off, then she added more briskly, "But I'm sure if you say you were here sleeping, that's exactly where you were."

Thanks a whole bunch, Nora thought resentfully and then quickly tried to tell herself that the housemother couldn't possibly have realized how damaging that sounded. "If you *say* you were here sleeping" . . . not, "Of course you were here sleeping."

"Let's just come along now, Miss," Sergeant Adelphi said, moving forward to take Nora's arm lightly. "No one's accusing you of anything. We just want to clear up a few details, that's all, and you might be able to help us do that. You *want* the Donner child found, right? I understand you two were pretty close. So I'm sure you're eager to help."

"Yes, of course I am. I just don't see how sitting around talking can help, if she's really lost."

"Oh, we don't think she's lost," Officer Blount said. Then his square, ruddy face changed expression, became grim. "We know for a fact that someone abducted the child from her backyard while the housekeeper was on the telephone."

His words hit Nora with all the force of a baseball bat against her temple. She gasped, wavered, leaned against the dresser for support. "Abducted? Kidnapped? You know for a fact that someone . . . someone *took* her?" she whispered, her face paper-white. "You mean . . . are you saying that Mindy has been kidnapped?"

"That's exactly what I'm saying. So you can see how serious this is. You can see why we need all the help we can get. You're not the only person we're talking to. There are others. So if you'll just come with us . . ."

Everything had changed so suddenly that Nora wasn't even sure exactly how it had happened. One minute, she'd thought they were talking about a child wandering out of her yard, and the next minute the horrible word "kidnapping" had snaked its way into her room.

Mindy? Kidnapped?

"I'll do anything I can to help," Nora said, and walked out of her room and down the stairs and through the foyer to the front door with the two officers. Then they all went outside and she climbed into the back seat of their car.

In the small, bright security office on campus, she described her Saturday over and over again until it began to sound even to her own ears as if she'd memorized it. As if it had been written down for her and all she'd had to do was learn her lines.

She could see by the expression on the officers' faces that they'd had the same thought.

There was so little to tell. She had, she told them, found another toy for Mindy that morning and decided to take it to her. The housekeeper, Mary, had left, Nora had stayed with Mindy, then the housekeeper had returned, and Nora had gone home in the throes of a migraine headache. Had taken two aspirin and gone straight to bed. Had been there ever since, hadn't even known Mindy was missing or that there was anything wrong. Had been *asleep*.

It sounded lame, even to her. But it was the *truth*.

The entire time that she was talking and repeatedly answering the same questions, maddening questions of her own were running through her mind, agonizing questions that the officers couldn't, or wouldn't, answer for her. When exactly had Mindy disappeared? Where was the housekeeper? Had she seen anyone approaching the house? Had any of the neighbors noticed anything suspicious? How was Mindy's father, Professor Donner, holding up?

Through a small window facing her, she watched a stream of familiar faces going in and out of the office across the hall. A tearful, pasty-faced Mary, glaring at her through the glass, then Helen Kieffer, her boss at the day care center, pointedly refusing to glance in Nora's direction. Helen was followed by a succession of employees of the center: Fitz, his thin shoulders hunched, his cheeks red because, Nora guessed, he knew she was in there and didn't want to look at her. Then Sabra Nicks, slightly taller than Nora but almost as thin, dark brown hair in braids. Sabra looked directly at Nora and gave her a friendly wave, as if to say, "Don't sweat it, it's no big deal."

"The housekeeper tells us," Officer Adelphi

said to Nora in a friendly voice, "that you were a little angry with the child this morning. That you yelled at her. Is that what happened?"

"Oh, no, I wasn't angry with *her*," Nora said hastily, feeling her face flushing with guilt. "It was the headache, that's all, and the heat. I'd never spoken to her sharply before, and it upset her. I felt really bad. But I couldn't stay to make it up to her because I was getting really sick."

Adelphi nodded and said, "Um-hum. Well, that can happen, can't it? Three-year-olds can be annoying, we all know that. And it's certainly easy to lose your temper when you're not feeling up to par, and it's hot as an oven out there." She glanced over at her partner, who was sitting opposite her at a small wooden table in the security office. Nora sat at the head of the table, facing both officers.

"But the thing is, Ms. Mulgrew," Adelphi continued, "we don't have a single person who can confirm that you actually were in bed, in your room, sleeping at the time the kidnapping took place. And we understand that the director of the day care center where you work, and where the Donner child is enrolled, had to warn you about becoming too emotionally involved with the child. Is that true?"

Nora felt sick. "Look, if I'd taken her," she said wearily, "where would I be hiding her? You were in my room at Nightingale Hall. There wasn't any little girl in there, was there?" Tears of anger, frustration, and fear stung her eyelids, but she was determined not to cry in front of these people. "Where is it that you think I've stashed Mindy?"

"If we knew that," Officer Blount said darkly, "we'd go get her, wouldn't we?"

Another blow, this one the harshest of all. It was the closest anyone had come to saying they actually believed that Nora Mulgrew had kidnapped Mindy Donner and was hiding her somewhere. Nora had never felt so totally alone in her life.

It seemed ironic to her that she felt alone, when there was a parade of her acquaintances flowing in and out of the office next door. After Sabra had come Lucas, short, stocky Lucas, with neatly combed blond hair and ruddy cheeks, looking healthy and fit, just the kind of person to become, one day, "the most famous pediatrician since Benjamin Spock." Nora didn't know Lucas that well, but it seemed to her that if that was what he wanted to be, that's what he would be. He seemed determined. He smiled at her, and waved. Amy Tarantino, small and dark-haired, came next. She'd been crying, Nora noticed, and she didn't smile when she glanced Nora's way. Nor did she wave. Amy was very fond of Mindy Donner.

This is ridiculous, Nora thought, watching them all come to tell everything they knew about Nora Mulgrew to anyone who asked. That wouldn't be much. She was glad now that she hadn't been friendlier. It gave them less ammunition to use against her. What did they know about her, anyway? Very little.

Nora Shane Mulgrew hadn't had an easy time of it. An only child, her adolescence had been marred by her mother's repeated hospitalizations in psychiatric facilities and then her death, followed fairly soon afterward by the death of Nora's father. They'd been told "heart attack," but Nora felt that her father had simply been too tired to continue living. He'd been worn out, after years of caring for an invalid wife and dealing with a daughter whose adolescence could only be called "emotionally charged." At least, that was what one high school counselor had called it. Nora, frightened that she had inherited her mother's emotional instability, had pulled herself together with sheer force of will, and resolved to stay out of the hospitals where her mother had so often been a patient. Except for one brief period, she had succeeded.

An unmarried aunt, Aunt Colleen, a school-teacher, had taken sixteen-year-old Nora in out of duty, not love. She'd made that very clear right from the start. As long as Nora kept to herself, did as she was told, and didn't upset the household in any way, the two lived in a cool but civil atmosphere in the cramped city apartment.

When Nora cried at her father's funeral, her aunt had awkwardly patted her on the arm and said, "Anything that doesn't break you makes you stronger, Nora. You remember that now."

So many things had happened to her, and she hadn't broken into pieces yet, had she? Except for that one time. So didn't that mean she was strong? Not frail, like her mother? She wanted to believe that. Needed to believe it.

Marjorie Dumas, blonde and heavyset, walked by, glowering at Nora as she passed the window. Marjorie adored Mindy Donner, and had resented Nora's friendship with the little girl. She had made no secret of her feelings. She'd done everything in her power to come between them, failing miserably.

I would love, Nora thought as Marjorie stomped sullenly past the window, to be a fly on the wall when Marjorie Dumas is asked questions about Nora Mulgrew.

Well, maybe not.

Nora had been slumped wearily in the hard-backed chair at the table. Now, she sat up very straight. Who *were* these people asking her all these questions, and asking other people questions about her, anyway? They weren't *real* police officers. They were campus security, employed to keep an eye out for theft and the occasional fistfight and any suspicious characters lurking about on campus. What did they know about a serious crime like kidnapping? Who did they think they were, the FBI?

"Do I need to stay here?" she asked sharply.

"No," Officer Adelphi said, shaking her head. "You can leave now. But don't go anywhere, okay? If that girl hasn't been found by tonight, we'll need to talk to you again."

Too many messages coming at her at once made Nora's head feel stuffed with cotton. Too much, too full, her head was too full. She couldn't think, couldn't get it all straight.

Snap out of it! she ordered silently, and began methodically sorting out the messages.

She could go. That was one message. A good message, a relief. A wonderful thing, being let go. But there was another message, this one a warning. They still suspected her, or they wouldn't be telling her not to leave town.

And there was still another message, a much more frightening one. "If that girl hasn't been found by tonight . . ."

Nora stood up. Her legs felt stiff and her back ached. There was a chance that Mindy wouldn't be found by tonight? The darkness of night might fall with Mindy still in the hands of the person who had snatched her out of her backyard? Oh, no, she'd be so scared. She was only three years old, and she, too, hadn't had such an easy time of it. How could someone do this?

Filled with a sudden, hot rage, Nora cried, "What is being done to *find* her? Is this all you're doing, sitting around asking innocent people stupid questions? Why aren't you out there *looking* for her?"

Officer Blount's face reddened and he was about to respond when Officer Adelphi said calmly, "Everyone's looking for her. Most of the other security officers, the Twin Falls police force, volunteers from campus and from town. Hundreds of people are looking for her. But," she added just as calmly, "if I were you, I don't think I'd volunteer right now."

That caught Nora by surprise. Of course she

was going to volunteer. She couldn't wait to get out there and join the search. She needed desperately to feel like she was doing something to help. "But you said I was free to go."

"You are. But we didn't question you without reason, Ms. Mulgrew. As we told you earlier, the housekeeper and some other people mentioned your name. You must know how rumors spread on campus. I'm afraid that if you went to the Donner house now, you wouldn't be welcomed with open arms. Go home, get some rest. There are plenty of people searching for the little girl."

Nora stared at her in horror. She wasn't going to be allowed to help search for Mindy?

Of course not. How could she have been so stupid? Hadn't the parade of day care workers passing by her window told her anything? By now, everyone on campus and in town knew Nora Mulgrew was suspected, at least a little, in the kidnapping of Mindy Donner. That kind of juicy rumor spread on campus like fire in an oil refinery. If even one person on campus said aloud that they thought she had done it, sooner or later everyone on campus would repeat what they'd heard, whether or not they believed it. Wasn't that the way rumors worked?

"I don't believe this is happening," Nora

murmured as she left the office. "I don't believe this!"

But the terrible truth was, she *did* believe it.

And she didn't know what to do about it.

Chapter 4

It was dark by the time Nora emerged from the security offices to a campus lit only by the round, old-fashioned globes marching on tall, black poles along the campus walkways. It was still hot, but a light breeze stirred the wisps of hair around her face.

She didn't know where to go. How could she sit in her room at Nightingale Hall knowing that Mindy was missing and she wasn't doing anything to help find her? But she knew the officer was right. Mary wouldn't let her in the front door, not after that look she'd given Nora when she passed by the window.

It was so unfair. If anyone wanted to find Mindy and return her to her father, it was Nora Mulgrew. And she wasn't going to be allowed to help.

"Nora?" A voice came out of the darkness from behind her.

Nora turned to see Lucas Grafton and Amy Tarantino standing under one of the pole lights. "Hi," Lucas said, approaching her, "we came to see if you wanted to go eat with us. You were in there so long, you must be starving. The volunteers looking for Mindy are taking their dinner breaks on shifts, and this is ours. Come with us."

They wanted her to go eat with them? But . . .

"Look," he said when they were standing in front of her, "we know you're not involved in this. So do Sabra and Fitz. They're waiting for us at Vinnie's. Come on, Nora, you have to eat."

Nora hesitated. His kindness touched her. He didn't know any more about her than anyone else did, but while others might be judging her unfairly, Lucas wasn't. But walk into a restaurant? Now? There would be stares, whispers.

Nora liked Vinnie's, a local pizzeria. It was a warm, welcoming, noisy restaurant that wrapped its arms around you the minute you walked in the door. It was always crowded, full of laughter and talk and music from the jukebox, and it smelled heavenly. If you didn't feel like eating, there was a poolroom at the back where people gathered, sometimes just to talk. She had gone there more than once when she really hadn't felt like company, just because it was such a nice place to be.

But now . . .

"Lucas is right," Amy said. Her eyes were still red and swollen from crying, but she sent Nora a weak smile. "You do have to eat. Vinnie's won't be crowded, because so many people are out searching. Anyway, you can't hide in your room, Nora. You haven't done anything wrong. Please come."

"I wasn't going to hide in my room," Nora said. "I want to look for Mindy."

The two exchanged an embarrassed glance.

"Okay, okay, I get the message!" She wasn't going to be allowed to help. "That housekeeper would never let me on the grounds, anyway." The bitter thought filled Nora with renewed anger.

She had so many questions. Why had the housekeeper implicated her? Had someone actually seen Mindy being taken from the yard? What was being done to find her? Lucas and Amy might be able to answer those questions for her.

Besides, why should she hide? Like Amy said, she hadn't done anything wrong.

Nora lifted her head and tightened her mouth. "Let's go eat!" she said defiantly. She would figure out a way to prove that she'd had nothing to do with Mindy's disappearance. Until then, she wasn't scurrying for cover like a criminal.

Her bravado lasted until they walked through the door of Vinnie's. The atmosphere was very different tonight. No music pouring from the jukebox, no laughter, very little chatter, and the restaurant's round tables were sparsely occupied. Instead of feeling warm and welcoming, the room was charged with tension and anxiety. Nora felt it the moment she walked in. And she felt that tension increase when heads looked up and people saw her standing in the doorway.

She kept her back straight, shoulders high, as she followed Lucas and Amy to the table in the center where Sabra and Fitz sat. If there were whispers, she couldn't hear them. But she could feel them, little insects of gossip flying around the room, stinging her, biting her skin, crawling up her back.

She did not sit with her back to the occupied tables. She faced them.

No one could answer her questions. She

found that out soon enough. All Lucas knew was that the housekeeper had told security about Nora showing up at the front door that morning with a toy for Mindy. "She said," Lucas told her when they had ordered, "that she let you play with Mindy for a while, and that she heard you yelling at her. She said that's when she came out and made you go home."

"I didn't yell at Mindy," Nora said, flushing angrily. "She was whining and I had a migraine, so I asked her to stop, that's all." She frowned. "Didn't the housekeeper tell security that she trusted me enough to let me stay with Mindy while she went next door?"

"She said she never left the house," Lucas answered.

Nora gasped. "That's *not true*! She went next door. And she was gone more than half an hour."

Amy shrugged. "She probably didn't want Professor Donner to know that she'd left Mindy alone. I mean," she added hastily, "with you. Afraid she'd get fired or something. So she didn't tell the truth."

"I don't see what difference that would make," Sabra said. "Whether the housekeeper left the house or not. Mindy wasn't taken while the housekeeper was gone, so it's not important, is it?"

"Of *course* it's important!" Nora said hotly. "It would tell the police that this morning at ten o'clock, the housekeeper didn't think I was a dangerous criminal. It would prove that I was with Mindy for over half an hour with no one else there. If I was going to kidnap her, that would have been the perfect time. So why didn't I? Why did I supposedly wait until later and return to the house to do it when the housekeeper was there? That doesn't make any sense. No wonder those security officers didn't believe anything I said. She's *lying*! She has to tell the truth." Her voice had risen. People were staring at her again.

"Nora, chill out," Sabra warned in a low voice. "You want people to think you've really lost it?"

Nora fell silent then, sinking back in her chair, fighting tears of frustration.

"I have to talk to that housekeeper," she murmured as their pizza arrived. "I have to make her tell the truth."

"Don't go over there," Fitz warned, selecting a steaming hot slice and placing it on Nora's plate. "Eat! Don't go near that place, and that's an order."

Nora didn't lift a hand toward her plate. "Why not? Would it look too much like the criminal returning to the scene of the crime?" she asked bitterly.

Fitz nodded. "That's exactly what it would look like. Besides, the housekeeper won't talk to you. She's come too close to accusing you outright. Stopped just short of saying she actually saw you carrying Mindy out of the yard."

Nora's anger simmered. She had never done anything to Mary except maybe inadvertently steal a little of Mindy's affection. Was that so terrible? It hadn't been deliberate. The punishment Mary had designed for her seemed much more severe than the innocent crime.

"Oh-oh, trouble approaching on the right!" Sabra murmured from behind a slice of pizza.

Nora looked to her right. Here came Marjorie Dumas, two friends in tow. Marjorie's eyes glittered, and her stocky form marched toward the table with a sense of purpose.

"So, Nora," she said when they arrived, "where are you hiding Mindy? What a dumb thing to do! You know the FBI will be called in if they don't find her tonight, right? You think you're so clever, you can mess with the FBI and get away with it?"

Nora didn't even look up. She kept her eyes on the center of the table, as if she were studying the pizza to see how it had been put together. "Go away, Marjorie. Crawl back into your dark little hole and don't come out until next spring."

Marjorie's round cheeks turned scarlet. "Very amusing. We'll see who's laughing when you get carted off to a jail cell. You wanted Mindy all to yourself, didn't you, Nora? Giving her all those presents, spending so much time with her, so the rest of us hardly got to play with her at all."

Nora sipped from her Coke glass, willing her hand not to shake. "You sound like a three-year-old yourself. What's wrong, none of the other kids will play with you? Small wonder." She spoke calmly, but inside she was seething. The quiet in the room had intensified and she knew people around them were listening to every word. It was humiliating.

"Well, we'll see," was all Marjorie could think of to say. She turned then and left, stomping out of the restaurant like the petulant child Nora had accused her of being.

Nora couldn't stand to sit there another minute. So many pairs of eyes staring at her, some disapproving, some curious, some laden with mistrust. She pushed her chair back and jumped to her feet. "Thanks for inviting me," she said, "but I've got to go. I . . . I have things to do."

"No, you don't," Fitz argued, looking up at her with concerned eyes. "Sit down."

"I'm going, too," Sabra said, standing up and brushing a lock of dark hair away from her face. "I hate not knowing what's going on. Is everybody else ready to leave? Maybe they've found Mindy by now. That would be good, right?"

"We'd have heard," Lucas pointed out. "Someone would have come in and announced it. No one has." But he, too, got up, a pizza slice in his hands. "I'm ready. I'll just take my portable meal with me."

Fitz and Amy decided to stay. "We've got ten minutes left on our break," Fitz said, "and I'm using them. Call me selfish, but I can't do my part if my stomach's empty, and I hate eating on the run. See you later."

There was a painful, awkward moment outside as Sabra and Lucas prepared to drive back to the search sites, and they realized that Nora couldn't go with them.

"I'm sorry, Nora," Sabra said, and Lucas nodded agreement.

"It's okay," Nora lied. "Really, I do have stuff to do. I'll keep the radio on so I'll know what's happening. Good luck, you guys. I'll . . . I'll keep my fingers crossed."

But she had every intention, as they waved good-bye and climbed into Lucas's car, of doing far more than that. Mindy Donner was missing, and Nora wasn't going to be sitting in her room at Nightingale Hall doing nothing more than crossing her stupid fingers.

When the car had pulled away and its lights had disappeared up the highway, Nora headed straight back to campus, walking fast along the road. The temperature had cooled enough to make walking possible without fear of another headache coming on. The sky overhead, clear that morning, was clouding up quickly.

Please don't let it rain, Nora prayed as she hurried along the berm, not with Mindy out there somewhere. Don't let it rain!

Once she got to campus, she went straight to the day care center. Closed on a Saturday evening, there would be no one there to shoo her away, to frown at her disapprovingly as she entered the front yard.

When she was standing inside the high, wooden fence, the yard filled with the shadowy bulk of a wooden playscape and sculpted, heavy stone dinosaurs in primary colors of red, yellow, green, and blue for the children to ride and sit on, Nora tried to think of why she had come here. Maybe some instinct had told her she might learn something here, something about why Mindy had been taken from her own yard.

She wouldn't have left with just anyone, Nora thought, moving around in front of the heavy wooden swing set to stand in the center of the lawn. Mindy was too smart for that. So the kidnapper had to be someone she knows well. Really well. The people who work here are the ones who know her best. She spends more time with us, with the staff here, than she does at home. She would have gone with one of us.

Who? Who did Mindy trust enough to reach up and take their hand and accompany them away from her own house?

It was very quiet at the center, a long, low building painted forest green, with pale yellow shutters and bright yellow front door. Works of art in fingerpaint and watercolor and crayon had been taped to the windows. The building was dark now, except for a light over the front door. Nora looked at it wistfully, wondering if she'd ever be allowed inside again. Her boss, Helen, would know now that she had visited Mindy at her house that morning. Visiting one of her young charges at home showed a definite disregard for Helen's warning not to "get involved." She wouldn't like it.

Nora half-turned, her eyes scanning the darkness for some sign, some clue, something to tell her she'd come to the right place, and as she turned, the silence was broken by a jingling sound and then by a faint swishing noise to her right. Her head automatically swiveled toward their source.

The heavy wooden swing came at her with great force, slamming into her right temple like a hammer. The blow knocked her off her feet and sideways. Her body landed on the soft, thick grass, but the back of her skull struck one of the heavy curved horns on the red stone stegosaurus directly behind her.

Without a sound, Nora's eyes closed and her body went limp.

Dispassionate eyes from beyond the swing

set watched without emotion as Nora flew backward and collided with the stone dinosaur.

Then, satisfied footsteps hurried away from the day care center.

Leaving Nora behind, unconscious.

Chapter 5

"Ah, I see you're awake. Good. We can get on with our story. I brought you some milk and cookies. You sit up and eat them like a nice girl and I'll sit here in the rocking chair and tell you more of my story.

"*The woman in the gray coat drove for a long, long time. The child cried until it fell asleep. When it woke up, it wasn't back home in its own bed. It was in a tiny cabin, set so far back into the woods that there wasn't even a road leading to it, only a rough trail created by the woman's truck. The woman's house wasn't big and roomy and bright with sunshine, like the house in the country with the pony and the rabbits. It was dark and dreary. And it was very cold, with a penetrating chill that made the child's bones ache.*

"*The cabin had no front porch where you could play on a rainy day. It had only two* steps made out of overturned wooden crates, leading to the door. Then you were inside. But the inside was only two rooms. One was a kitchen with a big old black stove and a sink on white metal legs underneath a small window curtained in red and white checks on one side, a sofa and an old faded brown chair and a low coffee table piled high with old magazines at the end closest to the front door.

"The other room was small, and very dim. There was a white iron bed surrounded by stacks of old books and magazines. There was a small, lumpy-looking cot stationed against one wall. Small twin windows sat very high in the wall so that no one could see in. The room smelled musty, as if the windows hadn't been opened in a long time, and that odor mixed unpleasantly with cooking smells because there was no door between the bedroom and the kitchen.

"There was no television set. Only a small, brown radio sitting on top of the refrigerator.

" 'It's not so bad, is it, precious child?' the woman asked. 'I tried to fix it up some. I made those pretty curtains you see at the window, bought the material in town and sewed them by hand. You'll sleep in my bedroom, on that nice little cot. Gets pretty cold in there sometimes, but I've got lots of quilts. Made those myself, too, out of scraps.' The woman laughed. 'That's one thing we've got plenty of around here, scraps. Most everything's scraps. But that's okay. We won't mind, will we? We'll have each other. Now, let's take your things off and get you settled.'

"The child cried and cried, for days, and begged the woman to take her home, but the woman always said the same thing, she always said, 'I've been alone too long. I don't have to be alone anymore, because I have you. This is your home now.'

"The child knew that it wasn't. Not this cold, tiny cabin with no other children to play with, no mommy and daddy, no rabbits, no pony, no other children. This wasn't home.

"Where were mommy and daddy? Why didn't they come to get their child?

" 'They don't want you anymore,' the woman said one night in a tired voice. 'I didn't want to tell you, but you just won't let up, you just won't stop that crying and whining and I can't stand it anymore, it's not supposed to be like this, we're supposed to be happy, just the two of us here in our little house. So I have to tell you. Your mommy and daddy asked me to take care of you because they only have enough time for one child and they wanted the other one the most. So they gave you to me. Forever.'

"At first, the child didn't believe it. Mommies and daddies didn't just give their children away. They wouldn't do that. Never, ever.

"But when many long days and nights had passed and no one came to take the child home, it seemed that maybe the woman was right. Maybe some mommies and daddies gave their children away.

"And the child knew why. Because it had temper tantrums, sometimes. And spilled things. And hadn't made its bed or hung its clothes up in the closet.

"Except . . . except the other child, the one they'd decided to keep, hadn't made its bed or hung up its clothes, either. And that child was still living in the big, sunny house, and riding the pony and playing with the rabbits. The child who hadn't called for help until it was too late was still living a fun, happy life with its mommy and daddy.

"It was so easy to figure out the truth, even at only five years old. That child hadn't called for help when the woman came out of the woods because it wanted everything for itself. It *wanted the older child gone, so that it could be the only child in the house, and would never have to share again.*

"When the older child figured out this horrible, terrible truth, it was filled with a furious, burning rage, so hot it made the hands shake, made the head dizzy, made the heart pound like a drum.

"On purpose . . . the younger child had let its sibling be kidnapped. It had been on purpose."

"I don't like this story. It's a gloomy gus story. That's what Norrie calls stories like what you tell. When dragons blow fire at peoples and the mean witch with the big ugly nose hides little kids, Norrie hates them stories. She don't tell them to me. You shouldn't, neither."

"Kiddo, I don't blame you for hating the story. I hated it, too, and I *lived* it. I brought you some books. I'll read to you. That'll be nice, won't it?

"The woman read books aloud. Grown-up books that the child didn't like and didn't understand until much later when the books were reread because there was nothing else to do.

"The child couldn't go to school because people would have asked questions.

"Had no friends, because there were none

out there in the deep, dark woods.

"There was no newspaper. No mail, ever. The woman was an obscure poet who earned a few dollars here and there publishing her poetry, but she had a post office box in town and picked up her tiny checks there.

"If it hadn't been for the radio and the piles of magazines that the woman bought when she took the truck into town once a month for supplies, the child would have had no sense of the outside world at all.

"The child was smart enough to know that the world was still out there, and the fierce rage inside grew with every passing day. "Might as well be raised by wolves," had been the grumbled comment at eight years of age. All hope of ever being rescued had long since vanished.

"The woman, her hair completely gray now, had taken offense at the remark. The next day, she had gone to town and returned with an armload of textbooks and a small, portable television set. She had set up a schedule, and began tutoring the child as best she could.

"The television set helped enormously, although the reception was poor. There were many nights when they couldn't watch it at all. Those were the worst nights. But on the good nights, the child saw a whole new world that *had been all but forgotten. Houses with people in them. Families laughing, arguing, doing things together. Children playing. How people looked, how they dressed, how they talked to each other.*

"Even the commercials were fascinating. There was so much that was unknown. A whole new world opened up through television. Would have watched it all day and all night if the woman hadn't insisted on the teaching hours.

"There was so little memory left now of the house in the country, of the mommy and daddy, of the sibling. Only distant images hiding somewhere in the back of the mind, too painful to be taken out and examined.

"The woman was never called 'Mom,' though it was what she wished for more than anything. They settled, finally, on 'Nana,' although when the child reached adolescence and its bitterness grew, it stopped using even that familiarity and called the old woman nothing but 'old woman.' "

When the child had nodded off again, her yellow curls spilling out across the white pillowcase like melted butter, she was left alone again, a second time, the door firmly closed and locked against intruders . . . or members of a search party seeking the small child.

The dark figure hurried away from the hiding place, its steps purposeful, as if it had someplace important to go, important things to do.

At the day care center, Nora awoke slowly. At first, when her eyes opened to darkness, she believed that she was in her room, lying on her bed. When she realized that she was lying on the ground, she remembered the heavy wooden rectangle coming at her out of the night, and she groaned aloud.

"She's coming to," a voice above her said.

The back of her head hurt even more than her temple did. She lifted a hand, gingerly touched the place beside her right eye that burned. Her fingers came away sticky. Blood. Her head was bleeding. She wasn't willing to try the same exploration on the back of her skull. That had been the blow that knocked her unconscious. She didn't even want to know what the damage was like back there.

But she did pull herself up to a sitting position.

"Ms. Mulgrew?" a deep but gentle voice said as someone knelt beside her. "I'm Officer Jonah

Reardon, Twin Falls police force. We got a call that you might be here. How badly are you hurt? Can you stand?"

Nora snapped to full consciousness. Police? Again? What did they think she had done now? "Yes, I can stand," she said curtly, only to find that when she tried, her knees buckled beneath her. An arm came out of the darkness to support her. She jerked away, annoyed, and that annoyance kept her upright.

A flashlight snapped on. She was looking then directly into the face of a tall, dark-haired officer who didn't look much older than she. Someone named Jonah Reardon. A police officer? Had he come to cart her off to jail?

But, he wasn't looking at her as if she were a criminal. What she saw in those dark eyes wasn't contempt or loathing, it was, she was sure, concern.

But there was another officer with him, a woman, who aimed her flashlight at Nora and said, "So. What were you doing here? Seems like a pretty odd place to be hanging out at night, wouldn't you say?"

"What did you mean, you got a call?" Nora asked as she steadied herself against the head of the red stegosaurus. "Someone called you and said I was here, at the center? Did they say that I'd been hurt?"

"Nope. Said you were hanging out here, that's all, and they thought we should know. After what happened to the little girl, and all."

"She wasn't taken from here. She was kidnapped from her own back yard. What does that have to do with the center?"

The woman shrugged broad, navy-blue-uniformed shoulders. "The kid was enrolled here, right? At this stage of the game, we're checking out everything and anything that could possibly be linked to her. Seems to us that a phone call about someone hanging out here, after dark, when it's closed, is worth checking out, don't you think, Ms. Mulgrew?"

Nora's fingers went absentmindedly to the gash at her temple, tiptoeing across it gently to probe its width and depth. Not too deep, but wider than she'd hoped. And still bleeding. She pulled a crumpled tissue from a pocket of her khaki shorts and dabbed at the wound carefully. "They haven't found Mindy yet?" she asked, deliberately directing her question toward the officer with the kinder expression on his face.

He shook his head. Someone had done a fine

job of sculpting the bones in his face. Unlike the dinosaurs scattered about the lawn, this face was well chiseled, with no lumps and bumps anywhere in sight. No mistakes at all. "We've been overloaded with phone calls," he said. "Sightings everywhere of a little toddler with blonde curls. But none of them panned out. People are still searching. What happened to your head?"

He had changed the subject so fast, Nora wasn't prepared for the question. "Oh . . . a swing." She pointed. "One of those swings came at me from out of nowhere. Slugged me and knocked me over, and then," pointing again, "I fell and hit my head on that."

He played his flashlight over the stegosaurus. A few strands of Nora's hair enmeshed in a thick blot of bright red adorned the horn that had knocked her out. "A swing? It's not windy. There's hardly a breeze at all."

"I think someone was there," she said, realizing for the first time that she did indeed think that. Like he said, there was no breeze. And that swing had come at her with enough force to knock her silly. No breeze would do that. "I think someone pushed it at me. Threw it, actually, as hard as they could."

"Why would someone do that?" he asked quietly, while the other officer's feet shifted impatiently.

"I don't know. But I know," Nora said, lifting her chin and looking him full in the face, "that someone did. On purpose."

"Any idea who this person was?" the female officer asked. And although she hadn't even hinted that she didn't believe Nora, disbelief sounded in her voice.

Like I would throw myself down on top of a stone stegosaurus and knock *myself* out, Nora thought, disgusted. "No," was all she said aloud. "Not the foggiest. Can I go now?"

"Reardon," the woman said crisply, "take her over to the infirmary and have someone take a look at that cut on her head. Then bring her back here. She never did tell us what she was doing here. In the meantime, I'm going to call for a team to go over this place with a fine-tooth comb."

Nora's jaw dropped. "Oh, you've got to be kidding! You think I'd hide Mindy *here* if I had her? Wouldn't that be totally stupid? Come Monday morning, that building will be overrun with staff and kids. Why on earth would I bring her here?"

The woman shrugged again. "A temporary measure, maybe? While the building's empty?

I can't say. And no one's accusing you, Ms. Mulgrew. If you're telling the truth about that swing being tossed at you, could be the person who threw it has the kid. All I know is, we have to check out every angle. If you really want the little girl found, I'd think you'd appreciate that."

"Come on," Reardon said before Nora could respond, "let's go have that head of yours looked at. I'll drive you."

"I can walk! It's not that far." But even as she said it and began walking, Nora was overcome by a feeling of dizziness so strong, her vision blurred. When it had cleared, she kept walking but said, as he walked alongside her, "Okay, then, drive me. But wait for me outside because I am *not* walking into the infirmary in the custody of a police officer."

"Sorry," he said, sincere regret in his voice. "Not possible. I have to stay with you, or Riley back there," nodding his head in the direction of the female officer, "will have my head. If anyone asks, we'll just say you had an accident. Nothing wrong with a police officer bringing in an accident victim, is there?"

How little he knew about campus gossip! But what choice did she have?

"So," he said when they were in the car and

moving across campus, "you really think you saw someone heave that swing in your direction?"

"I don't know," Nora answered, careful not to lean back against the seat. The thought of the wound at the back of her skull bumping against even something as soft as the upholstery of the seat, made her ill. "I'm not sure now. It was so dark . . ."

But that wasn't true. She *was* sure. The thick wooden swing, solid and hard as a boulder, had been thrown straight at her, deliberately, by someone she hadn't been able to see in the dark.

What she *wasn't* sure of was why someone would do that. That blow to her temple could have killed her.

Her stomach, already roiling from the blows to her head, churned more violently. *Killed* her? Could have *killed* her?

Yes. Could have, should have, would have if the blow had landed just a little harder. If she hadn't heard the chain jingling, hadn't turned fully around . . .

She would be dead now.

Chapter 6

The wound on the back of Nora's head required three stitches, while the abrasion at her temple was treated with antiseptic and a Band-Aid. The doctor urged her to stay the night for observation, but Nora refused. She wasn't ready to call it a night, not as long as Mindy was still missing.

"Going somewhere?" Officer Jonah Reardon asked as Nora emerged from the treatment cubicle and aimed straight down the hall toward the door.

Nora stopped. She'd forgotten about him. He was sitting on a plastic orange chair against the wall, twirling his navy-blue cap in his hands. "I'll give you a ride back to your dorm," he said, standing up and walking over to join her. "If that's where you're headed."

She could see in his eyes that he'd guessed she wasn't about to return to her room. She couldn't tell what he thought about it. "Don't you have someplace you need to be?" she asked archly. "Police business or something?"

"Can't leave yet. You haven't filled me in on what happened to you back there. At the center. We've already established that the wind didn't do it. So what was it that sent that swing flying into the side of your head? Or should I say, *who* was it? If you tell me, I won't have to take you back to Riley." He smiled. "She's a lot tougher than I am."

Nora turned and began walking. "I don't want to think about it. Why would someone deliberately try to split my skull in half? I don't have any enemies." Well, except for Mary. Hard to imagine her skulking around in the dark hurling swings at people.

"You must have at least one enemy," Reardon said, and followed Nora outside.

Thunder sounded in the distance. Nora thought immediately of Mindy. Was she inside somewhere? Was she terrified? Where *was* she?

"Talk to me, Nora," Reardon commanded, reaching out to halt her with a hand on her elbow. "I really do need some information here. I told the dispatcher at headquarters that I was taking an accident victim to the infirmary. I'll be expected to fill out a report. You have to give me something to put in it. Did you see anything, hear anything? What were you doing at the center?"

Nora shook his hand free and began walking again. "I don't know. I guess I thought there might be something there, some clue, anything . . ." Her voice faded as she remembered with a shudder that chunk of wood flying out of the darkness straight into her face. "Wasn't expecting to be ambushed, that's for sure." She glanced sideways at Officer Reardon. "You know some people are saying I took her, don't you? That I kidnapped Mindy? You must have heard."

"I heard." He returned her glance. "So, did you?"

"*No.*" They crossed the street to Reardon's police car.

"I didn't think so. Got any ideas who did?"

"None. Not a clue." Nora waited while he unlocked the door and opened it. She slid into the passenger's seat without argument. She would let him take her back to Nightingale Hall, and let him think she was going to bed. She could grab a raincoat while she was there, in case that thunder meant business. But the minute the taillights on his car had disappeared down the highway, she was out of there.

She talked about Mindy throughout the brief ride. How cute she was, how bright, how loving. "I just don't see how," she finished as Officer Reardon pulled up in front of the somber old house with the sagging front porch, "anyone could take such a sweet little girl away from her family like that. It's bad enough that her mother's in the hospital, but now this . . ."

Reardon got out of the car with her. "I've been here before," he said, his eyes on the house. "A while back. There was some trouble. You're not afraid to stay in a place everyone calls 'Nightmare Hall?' "

"No." But as she stood on the gravel driveway looking up at the dark brick structure, while flashes of silvery lightning lit up the woods behind the house from time to time, Nora was painfully conscious, for the first time, of a reluctance to go inside. The porch light wasn't on, and heavy draperies on the first floor windows hid the interior lights. The house looked completely deserted. The rooms upstairs would be dark and silent, the hall empty.

But wasn't that what she liked about her off-campus dorm? The solitude?

It *had* been. Now, she wasn't so sure. Things were different now. Someone at the day care center had sneaked up on her and tried to separate her left brain from her right brain. She didn't have a clue about who would do such a thing. More important, she didn't know where that person was *now*.

"Isn't there a barn out back?" Reardon asked, pointing.

Nora nodded. "Yeah, storage shed, really. The old barn burned, I heard. Supposedly, someone died in the fire."

"And who lives in that garage apartment?" He pointed to the two-story red garage that boasted a steep, narrow wooden staircase on one side, leading up to a door.

"The handyman, but he's not here. He's on vacation in Florida, which suits me fine. When he was here, he was forever painting something or hammering something."

The wind picked up suddenly, stirring the thick, gnarled branches of the huge, old oak trees shielding the house. The breeze cooled her skin, but signaled approaching rain. She was about to tell Officer Jonah Reardon good night and hurry inside when she heard him say, "Whoa, what's going on?"

Nora turned to see two police cars, their blue cartop lights revolving but their sirens silent, turning off the highway into Nightingale Hall's driveway.

Her heart thudded to a standstill. Mindy . . . something had happened . . . something bad? No! "Maybe they've found her! And they're coming to tell us."

"*Two* squad cars? I don't think so. Anyway, they could have given me that news over the radio. It's something else."

That sounded ominous to Nora. Something else? Meaning something *bad*.

Reardon walked over to greet the officers as they left their cars. Only one officer per vehicle. The rest of the force, Nora guessed, was busy searching for Mindy.

"This Ms. Mulgrew?" the taller officer asked Reardon.

"It is. Why?" Reardon walked back to stand beside Nora.

"Got a tip," the shorter, heavier policeman answered. He waved a piece of paper in the air. "Search warrant." To Nora, he said, "Need to check out your room, miss. If you'll be kind enough to lead the way."

"What are you searching for?" Jonah Reardon asked.

"Anything that might give us information on

the whereabouts of the Donner child."

"Well, you won't find that here," Nora said crisply. "I've already told you people everything I know. At least a dozen times."

"There isn't anything here," Reardon agreed. "She didn't take the kid."

"We got a tip, can't just ignore it," was the response. "The sooner we get to it, the sooner we'll be out of your hair."

Nora couldn't be sure if the noise she heard then was the rumbling of an approaching thunderstorm or the ominous sound of impending doom.

"What does he mean, a tip?" Nora asked Reardon quietly as they went up the porch steps ahead of the two police officers. "How could they be tipped off to something that isn't here? I don't have anything of Mindy's."

"Someone must have called and said you did. Don't worry about it. They'll look, they won't find anything, they'll leave. Relax!"

"You shouldn't have defended me out there," Nora added, keeping her voice low as she led the way up the stairs to the second floor. "You could get in trouble. Besides, how do you know I didn't do it? You don't know anything about me." She opened the door to her room and stood aside to let the officers pass.

Reardon, waiting in the doorway beside her, grinned. "I have a gift. A sixth sense. When I finish law school and pass the bar, it'll help me decide which cases to take and which ones to pass up. I'd take yours."

Overhearing, one officer, picking through the contents of Nora's trunk, called out, "Yeah, well you're not a legal eagle yet, hotshot. How about giving us a hand here?"

Nora stood in the doorway, arms folded across her chest, burning with rage and humiliation as the officers checked under her mattress, went through her dresser and desk drawers and her closet, even checking, she noticed with fury, the pockets of her jeans, raincoat, and two blazers.

"Don't you want to check the fillings in my teeth?" she asked sarcastically when she could restrain herself no longer.

They ignored her, although Reardon sent her an understanding glance.

The phone rang.

"Am I permitted to answer my own phone, or were you about to take it apart to make sure I'm not hiding Mindy in the receiver?" Nora asked even as she defiantly walked to the phone and yanked it off the hook.

"Hello?"

"Kid-snatcher!" a voice hissed in Nora's ear. "Kid-snatcher! I hope you get the death penalty! I hope you fry!"

Click.

For several seconds after the line went dead, Nora clung to the receiver, unable to believe she'd heard correctly. "Kid-snatcher"? Her?

She dropped the phone back into its cradle.

Reardon was just passing, carrying a half-full wicker wastebasket. When he noticed the expression on her face, he stopped. "What? What's wrong? Did they find her?"

Mute, she shook her head. "Wrong number," she finally managed. "Happens all the time."

She could tell he didn't believe her. But he didn't argue. He turned and walked away, the wastebasket still in his hands.

And a few minutes later, he said in an odd voice, "Ms. Mulgrew?"

When she turned around, he was holding up a candy box. A pink ribbon still sat atop the lid, which was raised. Reardon's eyes were on the contents.

The other two officers arrived at Reardon's side at the same moment as Nora. Three pairs of eyes looked down into the box.

It held fingernail clippings.

Ten of them.

Ten clippings, neat and precisely cut, from ten very small fingernails.

Fuchsia in color. Bright, vivid fuchsia, carefully applied, with no smearing at the edges.

I tried to talk her into Powder Puff Pink, Nora's shocked mind remembered. But she insisted on Thunder Alley Fuchsia.

She had painted Mindy's fingernails with Thunder Alley Fuchsia on the morning of the day before she disappeared.

And now the tips of those same fingernails, the polish not even chipped yet, were lying in an old candy box discovered in her room.

The phone rang again.

Chapter 7

No one moved to answer the ringing telephone. It shrilled four times and then fell silent.

"That's not mine," Nora said finally. "That box doesn't belong to me. In my entire life, no one has ever sent me candy." Then, feeling Officer Reardon's eyes on her, she flushed, embarrassed. What a stupid thing to say. He wasn't feeling sorry for her, was he? It wasn't as if she'd been complaining. She had said it only to fortify her claim that the box, with its disgusting contents, couldn't possibly belong to her.

"We don't care about the box," one of the officers said. "Only what's inside. Unless I miss my guess, those clippings are from a little kid's fingernails. Someone, say, about the age and size of the Donner girl."

"I didn't put those in there!" Nora insisted,

backing away from the box. "Someone else did."

"Right." The officer slid the box and its contents into a clear plastic bag. "We'll just take this into town and have the lab check it out."

"You'll be available, right?" the other officer asked Nora as the pair turned to leave.

"Am I under arrest or not?" Nora asked.

"Not yet," she was told by one of the departing officers. "Have to check out this box first. Just don't be taking off on us, hear?"

As the officers were about to leave Reardon directed his dark brown eyes on Nora. "You sure you'll be okay here alone?" His gaze moved to the Band-Aid across her temple.

I won't be here alone, Nora thought, because I won't be here at all. Aloud, she said, "Yes. I'll be fine." Then she added anxiously, "You'll call me the minute you find her?"

Reardon opened the door. "I'll do better than that. I'll come here in person to give you the good news. Don't worry, okay? We'll find her."

Nice of him, Nora thought as the door closed after him. She still didn't understand why he was being so decent to her when he didn't know her any better than the other policemen did.

That "sixth sense" of his, telling him she was innocent? Maybe.

Too bad he was a cop and would probably be carting her off to jail any minute now.

She stood at the window watching until all three police cars had disappeared from sight. Then she grabbed her blue raincoat and left the room.

Once outside, she hesitated on the wide, stone steps. Which way to go?

She knew from Reardon that the search parties were concentrated on campus. She would have to avoid that area. She wouldn't be welcome there. Besides, the nasty phone caller could be one of the searchers. The thought of running into him in person made her skin crawl.

Why did everyone assume that the kidnapper was hiding Mindy on campus? If *I* had taken her, the way everyone thinks I did, Nora thought as she moved down the steps, the first thing I would have done was get her away from campus where everyone knows her.

And take her where?

To know that, Nora decided, you would have to know *why* Mindy had been taken in the first place. Not for ransom. Professors didn't make that kind of money, and right now most of Professor Donner's money must be going for medical bills. Anyone who knew Mindy well enough that she would walk off with them had to know the professor's economic situation.

Then *why* had Mindy been taken?

A sudden sound behind her brought Nora's head up. Mrs. Coates was out for the evening. Wouldn't have been wandering around outside even if she had been home. The police officers were gone. There should have been no sound anywhere on the hill except the soft whisper of her own breathing and the gentle tap of the wind on the oak leaves overhead. The threatened rain hadn't materialized.

Nora's heart skipped a beat. The voice on the phone calling her a "kid-snatcher" had known where to reach her. Knew where she lived.

He was sick, or he never would have delivered such a cruel message.

What would he do to her if he found her?

Nora lifted her face and listened carefully. But she heard nothing but the wind and the erratic beating of her own heart.

Relieved, she began walking away from the house, pulling her hood over her hair. She had taken only a few steps when darkness completely enveloped her and she realized her mistake. She had left the house without a flash-light.

Duh. "Planning to conduct a search in the dark without a light of any kind, are you, Nora?" she muttered, and was about to retrace her steps when it struck her that she was now closer to the cellar entrance than to the front of the house. There would be a flashlight or lantern in the cellar, where the handyman kept all of his tools. She could borrow one, if the slanted wooden doors set into the ground weren't locked.

When Nora walked over and bent to tug on one, it opened. It was heavy, but when she used both hands, she was able to set it aside. What looked like a giant black pit lay below her, as if waiting to swallow her up.

Nora had never been in Nightingale Hall's cellar. Had never had any reason to be.

Cool, damp air floated up to her from the opening, and a musty, moldy smell came with it. It didn't look very inviting.

But she needed a flashlight.

She felt her way down the stone steps into the black, musty void, and stood for a few seconds on the earthen floor just inside the door-way. The cellar was wide and low-ceilinged, with shadowy, bulky shapes looming out of the darkness here and there. One was ⟨...⟩ fashioned furnace, Nora decided. The res⟨...⟩ boxes and trunks and old furniture. She cou⟨...⟩ feel the dampness of the cellar seeping through her clothes, and fought the urge to turn and hurry back up the steps.

When her eyes had become accustomed to the lack of light, she made her way to a long, high, wooden bench against one wall, and fumbled among the tools there until her fingers closed around what felt like a flashlight. She flicked the switch, but nothing happened.

"Nor-rie!"

Hands on the flashlight froze.

"Nor-rie, where are you?" The voice was distant, eerie, as if it were coming from far away, but the words were clear and distinct, mournfully wailed in a child's sweet voice. *"Norrie! Come and get me. I want to go home!"*

Nora whirled away from the bench, her breath catching in her throat. "Mindy?" It came out a hoarse whisper. She cleared her throat, tried again, louder this time. "Mindy? Is that you?"

"Norrie, please come take me home. I want my daddy."

Nora's eyes frantically scanned all four corners of the cellar. "Mindy, where are you?"

"Here, Norrie, I'm here!" But the voice was too faint to reveal its location.

Nora took a hesitant step forward. She had completely forgotten about the flashlight. "Mindy, tell me where you are. Tell me where you *are!*"

But when the voice came again, it was fainter, and fading fast.

The voice was too distant now to still be in the cellar. Nora stumbled forward, toward the entrance. "Mindy, don't go! Stay there, so I can find you. Wait, wait!" She reached the doorway, plunged up the steps, repeatedly shouting Mindy's name.

But she emerged at the top of the steps into total silence. The childish voice was gone.

Nora wasn't willing to give up. To have Mindy so close, so close, only to lose her again was more than she could stand.

Panic took over then. Nora began running through the dark night, shouting the child's name. As she ran, first around the house to the back, then toward the new barn sitting on the edge of the steep, wooded hill, her mind raced along with her feet.

She's here somewhere, somewhere on this hill, I have to find her, take her home, she'll be safe there, she's counting on me . . .

When, breathless, she reached the new barn, she skidded to a stop just before the wide, double doors and stared at it. The barn?

Why not? Wouldn't it be a perfect place to hide someone? Besides, the new structure sat far enough away from the house that a small child's voice wasn't likely to carry that great a distance.

But *I* heard her, Nora thought, puzzled.

"Nor-rie! Where are you?"

Nora snapped to attention. The plaintive wail was definitely coming from inside the barn.

Call for help, an inner voice warned. Mindy didn't go in there alone. Someone *took* her in there. Someone cruel enough to kidnap a child, think what he might do to *you*. Call Officer Reardon, wait for him, and then the two of you can go inside together.

"Norrie!"

Impossible to take the time to run all the way back to Nightingale Hall, go inside, make the phone call, then wait for Reardon. Couldn't be done, not with Mindy crying out like that. Find her first, make sure she's safe, then make the call. Had to be done that way. No choice.

Making up her mind, Nora pushed aside the wide, flat board barring the entrance of the new barn, and slid one side of the door open.

"Mindy? Are you in here?"

No answer.

Nora took a few cautious steps inside, and as she did, a new thought emboldened her, eased her fear: Mindy had to be alone. Her captor would never have let her yell for help, would have silenced her after the very first cry. He must have gone off and left the child, knowing that Mindy was too tiny to slide the heavy door open.

"Mindy, it's Nora. I'm here. It's okay, honey. Just tell me where you are, and I'll come and get you."

No answer.

The faint outline of a wooden platform three-quarters of the way up one wall drew Nora's attention upward. A hayloft.

Nora moved farther on into the barn, her eyes fixed on the loft and the wooden ladder leaning against its edge. "Mindy? Are you up there?"

The voice that answered her then was not the sweet, distressed cry of a child. It was deeper, harsher, and laden with cruel glee. "No, but *I* am!" The shout was followed by wild, maniacal laughter, shrill and blood-curdling, fouling the air in the barn like toxic smoke. Just as quickly, it changed, sounding now identical to the cries that had brought Nora into the barn. "Oh, Nor-rie," the falsely childlike voice begged softly, "come and get me, Norrie, come and save me from the big, bad kidnapper."

"It was *you*," Nora breathed, her head still uptilted, her feet beginning to back away from the loft. Her spine collided with a wooden post in the center of the barn. She stayed there, grateful for the support now that fear was turning her legs to mush. "Mindy wasn't calling me. *You* were!" Her voice shook as she added, "What have you done with her?"

"That's for me to know and you to find out." There was thinly disguised glee in the voice.

"Why are you *doing* this?" Nora screamed.

"Do unto others," a thin falsetto answered, "as they have done unto you. That's my motto!"

"Mindy couldn't possibly have done anything to you. She's only a little girl." Nora peered up into the loft, trying to make out a shape . . . height, weight, or colors . . . hair, clothing, anything to tell her who the disembodied voice belonged to. But she could see nothing. It wasn't even possible to guess gender, the way the voice kept changing.

"Never assume that all children are innocent

little angels," the voice said harshly. "It's not true. Don't make that mistake." Then, in a different, almost-giddy voice, it cried, "Look out below!" and an object came whizzing through the air straight at Nora.

Just before it ripped into her, one of the sharp tines slicing through her raincoat and penetrating the flesh of her upper right arm, Nora recognized the size and form of the object hurled at her from the hayloft as a pitchfork.

There was no time to throw herself out of the way. The tine caught her with a blow forceful enough to slam her back against the post. She felt the sharp, stabbing sensation in her right arm and then the wound on the back of her head, the skin held together with new stitches, collided with the heavy wooden post. The pain was so great, she had to bite down hard on her lower lip to keep from losing consciousness.

But, though her knees buckled and she sank to the wooden floor, kneeling, something kept her alert. She didn't know if she stayed conscious out of stubbornness, or fear that if she fainted, he would finish her off. Her eyes remained open, and her mind continued to function. Gritting her teeth, she reached over and yanked the pitchfork out of her right arm, then twisted it around in front of her to use as a weapon if she needed it. It seemed unusually small, but it was all she had.

"Go ahead," she gasped, her eyes on the loft, "come on, come down where I can see you. Show your face, coward!"

She heard a scrambling sound up above, and although she could see nothing but a shadow, her eyes followed the form as it scrambled along the platform to a small, oval door at one end, facing Nightingale Hall. Fingers reached up, undid the latch. Hands pushed the little door open. The figure hoisted itself up and out and over the edge, and disappeared. She heard a grunt and a soft thud as it hit the ground, and for one small, terrifying moment, she expected to see someone approaching the open door to the barn and coming at her.

Instead, she heard more scrambling sounds, then the unmistakable thud of footsteps as feet hurried away from the barn.

She was alone again.

And she was still alive.

Chapter 8

Crouching at the base of the wooden post, Nora waited, paralyzed with fear, still expecting the figure to appear in the wide doorway and rush toward her to finish her off.

But when a shadowy figure did appear, a voice quickly said, "Nora? Is that you?"

"Lucas!" Nora climbed shakily to her feet. "Lucas, did you see him? He must have passed you. He just left!"

Lucas wasn't alone. Amy, Sabra, and Fitz were right behind him. Fitz carried a large flashlight. Its beam lit up most of the barn. "Did I see who?" Lucas asked as they all arrived at Nora's side. "Who just left? And what are you doing with that pitchfork?"

"The kidnapper, that's who," Nora answered the first question. "He must have gone right by you. He was up in the loft." She pointed. All eyes followed her trembling hand. "He threw this pitchfork at me." She looked down at the fork she was holding. Under the flashlight's glow, she could see that the tool *was* small, clearly built for children's hands. But it wasn't a toy. The tines were made of strong metal, not plastic. And it hadn't felt like a toy when it impaled her arm.

"Did it hit you in the arm?" Sabra asked, pointing. "It's bleeding, and your raincoat is torn."

"Yes. He threw it at me, and then he jumped out that little door at the end of the loft. I thought he was coming back in here to finish the job, but you guys showed up instead."

All eyes returned to the shadowed hayloft.

"What's going on here?" Officer Jonah Reardon's voice said as he entered the barn. He had returned to inform her there were no fingerprints on the box of nail clippings, not even hers, which meant that she wasn't under arrest . . . for now. He listened attentively as she told him what had happened.

"Take her inside," Reardon told the others when Nora had finished her frightening story. "If Mrs. Coates is home, have her take a look at that arm. That looks nasty. I'll check out the loft. See what I can find."

On the way to the house, Nora said, "I

thought you guys were looking for Mindy. What are you doing here? Has she been found?"

Lucas shook his head. "Not yet. Wish I could tell you different, but I can't. We decided to meet here so we could check up on you. Our shift is over. Another team has taken over."

Fitz held the back door open. "We didn't expect to find you in the barn with a pitchfork in your hands. You sure you're okay?"

Nora had no idea if she was okay or not. It didn't seem important. "I can't believe none of you saw him," she complained, sitting down in one of the wooden kitchen chairs. "Where could he have gone when he jumped from the hayloft?"

"Into the woods, maybe," Amy suggested, taking a seat opposite Nora. Her dark, curly hair, rain-moistened, clung to her forehead and cheeks. "He could have disappeared into the trees and undergrowth just as I came around the house."

Nora frowned. "Weren't you all together? Didn't you get here at the same time?"

"No." Fitz pulled up a chair next to Amy. "We were all on separate search teams. But we arranged to meet here when we were re-placed by a fresh team. So, tell us again what you were doing out in the barn."

Amy and Sabra went in search of the house-mother while Nora repeated the sequence of events. When Mrs. Coates arrived, in robe and slippers, pink foam rollers in her hair, she disinfected and bandaged Nora's arm. The puncture wound hurt, but the sharp metal tine had missed the bone.

"If that really was the kidnapper in the barn with you," Amy said thoughtfully, "then . . . where was Mindy?"

A sobering question, and an important one.

"Tied up, maybe?" Lucas ventured when Nora didn't answer. "Or locked in somewhere?"

The images his suggestions conjured up were distasteful to all of them. Clever, adorable Mindy, tied up, maybe gagged?

Perhaps to offset the frightening pictures torturing all of them, Fitz said, "Maybe that *wasn't* Mindy's kidnapper in the barn, Nora. Maybe it was somebody else, someone with a really sick sense of humor. I've read about people like that in other kidnappings . . . the lunatic fringe who take advantage of someone's misery to get attention."

Nora's mind heard again the telephoned accusation: "Kid-snatcher!" Doubt swept over her. She'd been so sure the voice in the barn had belonged to Mindy's captor. "But he faked

Mindy's voice," she protested aloud. "Why would he do that, if he wasn't involved in the kidnapping?"

Fitz shrugged. "Like I said, the lunatic fringe. Everyone knows she's missing, anyway. And anyone can imitate a kid's voice. It's easy."

"You know, Nora," Amy added reluctantly, "a lot of people on campus think *you* took Mindy because you were so attached to her and kept saying you'd always wanted a sister. Other people say you did it to get back at Helen for lecturing you in front of everyone last week. Telling you not to spend so much time with Mindy. Maybe the guy in the barn was one of those people."

"Cut it out, Amy!" Sabra said sharply. "You're scaring Nora."

"Oh, I'm scared, all right," Nora admitted, standing up. "Which is why I'm going to my room right now. Maybe I'll feel safe there. But it's not Amy who's scaring me. It's . . . it's everything."

"We'll come with you," Lucas offered. "And wait with you until that cop comes back and tells us if he found anything in the hayloft."

Any other time, Nora would have declined

their company, sent them away. But not to-night. Tonight, she was in no hurry to be alone.

All the way up the stairs, Lucas and Fitz made half-joking comments about the "creepy atmosphere" in Nightingale Hall, and Sabra said, "No wonder they call it Nightmare Hall. The perfect name, if you ask me."

Nora didn't argue. It *was* beginning to seem like the perfect name.

She was in such a hurry to return to the safety of her room that she never saw the note.

It was Amy who found it, lying just inside Nora's door. "Nora?" She bent to pick up the piece of paper. "Someone left you a message."

The only friends Nora had on campus were already with her, here, in this room. If one of them had slid the note under the door, they would be saying so, now. Lucas or Sabra or Fitz would see the note in Amy's hand and one of them would say, "Oh, that's mine. I left it earlier, Nora. You must have already gone out to the barn."

But no one said that.

"Nora?" Amy repeated, extending the note.

"Don't read it!" Nora said frantically. "Don't look at it, throw it out."

But Amy was already looking down, already

reading aloud. GIVE THE KID BACK OR YOUR LIFE WON'T BE WORTH TWO CENTS!

It was signed, A FRIEND TO ALL CHILDREN EVERYWHERE.

Amy finished reading and lifted her head, her dark eyes wide with chagrin. "Oh, Nora, I'm sorry. You were right. I shouldn't have read it."

"Yes," Fitz said, walking over to take the note from Amy's hand, "you should have." He scanned the paper quickly, then tossed it into the wicker wastebasket. "It's like I said, Nora. Some sicko, torturing you. Probably the same creep who was in the barn."

"I don't think you should throw that note away," Lucas said, striding over to the basket to pluck free the offending piece of paper. "We can give it to that cop when he comes . . . whoa, what's *this*?"

Nora, sitting on her bed, looked up at the change in his tone of voice.

Lucas was holding the crumpled piece of paper in his left hand. In his right, he held a small pink shoe.

A sneaker.

A very small sneaker.

A very small pink sneaker, with Velcro fasteners for little fingers that had not yet conquered the intricacies of tying laces.

Nora recognized the shoe immediately.

So did Amy and Sabra. "That's Mindy's!" they breathed almost simultaneously.

"No," Nora said in a flat voice, standing up, her hands at her mouth, "no, it can't be! Not in my wastebasket, in my room, it's not, it's *not*!"

"Probably another sick joke," Fitz said. "It's disgusting, that's what it is."

Sabra reached out then to take the shoe from Lucas. She glanced inside the small, pink sneaker. "It's Mindy's, all right," she said, looking up to meet Nora's eyes. "Her name tag's inside. M.L.D. Mindy Louise Donner. Mindy."

No one said a word.

A few silent seconds later, Jonah Reardon's voice said, "What's going on?" Fitz had left the door open and Reardon had walked in without knocking. "Sorry I was gone so long," he said. "Hated to give up. But I didn't find a thing."

After a moment's hesitation, Lucas said, "*We* did." He held up the note and the sneaker.

"It's hers?" the officer asked, moving forward to take the shoe from Lucas. "Where'd you find it?"

"In my wastebasket," Nora answered. She didn't like the way the other four were looking at her. They'd been supportive up until now, far more so than she would have expected, considering how little they knew of her. But now she could see new questions in their eyes. They were as stunned by the discovery of the shoe as she was, but she had an advantage over them. She *knew* she had never put that shoe there. They couldn't know that, not really.

"Anyone could have put this shoe here, Nora," Jonah Reardon surprised her by saying. "In fact, if someone is trying to throw suspicion your way, and the box of fingernail clippings suggests just that, this really was a pretty dumb move. He's expecting the police to believe that you'd be stupid enough to leave this kind of evidence lying around if you were the real kidnapper?"

"It wasn't exactly lying around, officer," Amy pointed out. "It was sort of hidden in Nora's wastebasket."

"It wasn't hidden, Amy," Lucas disagreed. "I saw it right away."

"Sorry," Amy apologized, flushing slightly. "I didn't mean that the way it sounded."

But Nora wasn't convinced. It had sounded

to her as if Amy had said exactly what she'd been thinking.

"Look," Reardon said, "I'll have to take the shoe downtown. And the note. The captain needs to know about these things. But I checked that wastebasket myself today and there was no shoe in it then. Seems pretty obvious to me that it was planted there."

Buoyed by his support, Nora showed him the child's pitchfork. "First a swing," he murmured, "now a child's gardening tool. Whoever is doing this wants to make sure the message is clear, right? That his attacks are somehow connected to the Donner girl's disappearance?"

"Couldn't it just be someone who *thinks* Nora is guilty and is trying to punish her, like the note implies?" Fitz asked.

Reardon nodded. "Could be. But there's been no announcement in the media about any suspects at all, so it would have to be someone from campus, someone who's heard the rumors. Anyone got any ideas?"

They all exchanged dubious glances and shrugged.

"I don't understand what's going on," Nora said in a dull, emotionless voice. She was so tired, and she especially hated having attention focused on her when everyone's energy should be concentrated on finding Mindy.

"I don't, either," Amy echoed.

"*You*," Reardon said to Nora, "are staying in this room. Get some sleep. I'm going to take this stuff to the station. Lock the door when we leave. It's late, and there's no place you need to go. I'm coming back here when I've turned this stuff in," holding up the shoe and the note, "to make sure you stay put."

"I don't need police protection," Nora argued. "You should be out looking for Mindy, not playing guardian angel to me. I'm fine." The throbbing in her injured arm and the knot on the back of her head disagreed with her, but she ignored them. "Besides, if you park that police car in front of Nightingale Hall, everyone passing by will think it's because I'm a suspect. They'll think you're making sure I don't try to escape."

"Maybe. But the loose cannon who used you for pitchfork target practice in the barn will see the car, too. And he'll think twice about coming after you again."

When he had gone, the heels of his boots echoing sharply along the hall until he hit the carpeted stairs, Amy turned to Nora and said, "Well, your own personal protector! Good going, Nora. And he's cute! Where'd you find him?"

"I didn't find him. He found me." Nora told them about the runaway swing at the day care center. "The weird thing," she added, sitting back down on her bed, "is that he seems pretty sure that I didn't snatch Mindy. I mean, I'm grateful, but I don't get it. He hardly knows me."

"Well," Lucas said loyally, "we don't know you very well, either, but *we* know you didn't do it."

Nora waited for loud, enthusiastic agreement from the other three. It didn't come, although they did nod almost automatically.

Never mind. She had other things to think about. "They'll keep searching all night long, won't they?" Her head was throbbing wickedly now. She needed to sleep. But how could she do that with Mindy still missing?

"All night," Fitz confirmed.

"They replaced us," Amy told Nora, "because they wanted teams that weren't too tired to be alert. We're supposed to go home and sleep and go back in the morning."

Nora looked so stricken at the thought that Mindy might not have been found by morning, that Lucas quickly amended, "But I'm sure they'll have found her by then, Nora. They will."

Promising to call her the minute they heard anything, the four left.

Nightingale Hall seemed more deserted than it ever had when they had gone. Nora had always liked the peace and quiet of the house. She had valued it. Now she was beginning to fear and despise it.

She locked the door, turned off the light, and retreated to her bed. It was still raining lightly outside, the drops making a faint rapping sound against the glass of her open window.

Nora lay on her back, staring up at the ceiling. How had Mindy's sneaker made its way into Nora Mulgrew's wastebasket! Was it really Mindy's shoe? Anyone could put a name tag into a pink sneaker. Was it supposed to be another message, like the sinister note and phone call? Or was it just another attempt to make her look guilty, like the box of fingernail clippings?

If that really was Mindy's shoe, and she'd been wearing it when she was taken, only one person could have placed it in the wastebasket. The real kidnapper.

Nora fought the impulse to phone Mary at the Donner house and ask which shoes Mindy had been wearing that day. She had more than one pair. It seemed like a really important question.

But even if the housekeeper were willing to answer the question, it was much too late to call now. It would have to wait until morning.

The kidnapping, and the attacks on her at the day care center and again in the barn were connected, Nora was convinced of that. She didn't know how or why, but she knew they were.

Her head began to throb viciously. Oh no, not another migraine.

Nora wrestled with her fear and worry over Mindy until the first faint rays of dawn turned her room a smoky silver. Then, against her will, her eyes closed and she sank into an exhausted, fitful sleep.

In her sleep, she heard again the taunting, falsetto voice calling her name repeatedly.

So when she awakened to a room filled with bright sunshine and heard her name being shouted, it took her a while to realize that she was awake, she wasn't dreaming, and someone really was calling her name. From outside.

That same someone was pounding ferociously on Nightingale Hall's front door.

Chapter 9

Nora bolted upright in bed. Someone was pounding on the front door and shouting her name. It was Sunday morning. Mrs. Coates went to church on Sunday. She never locked the front door. If Lucas, Amy, Sabra, or Fitz had come rushing to Nightingale Hall to present the good news that Mindy had been found, they would have burst into the house without knocking and run right up to her room.

So it wasn't any of them shouting her name on the front porch.

But that didn't mean it couldn't be good news. Jonah Reardon had promised to let her know when Mindy had been found. Maybe that was him on the front porch yelling up at her to let him in.

Nora jumped out of bed and yanked on shorts and a T-shirt. "I'm coming!" she shouted out the open window, but the pounding continued.

She ran down the stairs, fingers on both hands crossed behind her back. "Please, please, please!" she whispered as she hurried to the front door. "Let this be Jonah Reardon, smiling and telling me that Mindy is home, safe and sound, where she belongs."

She yanked the door wide open.

The man who had been pounding so frantically and shouting Nora's name was Professor Keith Donner. Mindy's father.

He looked terrible. He was ordinarily a nice-looking man. Now, his eyes were red-rimmed from lack of sleep, he needed a shave, his thinning dark hair was uncombed, his face pale and drawn. "Do you know where my daughter is?" he asked Nora in a hoarse, shaky voice. "*Do* you? If you do, please tell me, please!"

Nora was too startled to speak at first. Then, when she realized what he had said, too horrified.

"If you know anything, anything at all," Professor Donner continued, brushing past Nora to stand in the entry hall, "you have to tell me." His tan slacks were wrinkled, as if he'd slept in them, his white shirt dotted with coffee stains from cups held with trembling hands.

But it was his eyes that made Nora bleed inside. They were tortured, filled with panic and fear for his missing child.

"I don't know anything, Professor Donner," she answered, struggling to keep the hurt out of her voice. She couldn't blame the distraught man for clutching at straws. But he had to know that if she had the tiniest bit of information about Mindy, she'd tell. He just wasn't thinking straight in his terror for his daughter. "I wish I did, but . . ."

"I don't believe you."

The statement, uttered in a low, desperate voice, caught Nora off guard. Then, when the words sank in, her jaw dropped, and she stared at him, thinking that perhaps she hadn't heard him correctly. "Excuse me?"

"*I said,* I don't believe you. I overheard some of the searchers talking. Your name kept coming up. And I know how attached you were to my little girl." His voice broke, then gained strength again. "I thought it was a *good* thing, you giving her special attention, visiting her at the house, giving her those toys, while her mother was in the hospital. A good thing. But now I think you decided she was being neglected, not getting enough attention while her mother is sick, and that upset you, so you took her from us." The hot sun was shining directly down upon the front of the house. Beads of perspiration dotted the professor's forehead. "If you did that, Nora, you have to tell me. You have to tell me where you've hidden her. I won't press charges, I give you my word, I know you thought you were doing the right thing for Mindy." He was pleading now, begging. "But she belongs at home, Nora, you know that, you know she does. Just tell me where you're hiding her. I'll go get her, and I won't even tell the police where I found her. I just want her *back*. They won't know anything, I promise."

"Professor Donner," she said, willing her voice to remain as steady as possible because anything else might make her seem guilty, "I do *not* know where Mindy is or who took her. If I did, I would tell you. I want her found as much as you do." She would have added, "Maybe more, since that's the only way I'm going to get out from under this nasty cloud of suspicion," but looking into his anguished eyes, she realized there wasn't anyone on earth, not even her, who wanted Mindy Donner found, safe, more than the child's father.

"I would never have taken Mindy away,

never!" she cried when the expression on his face didn't change.

She waited for him to believe her, to hear the sincerity in her voice, to remember that she loved Mindy and Mindy loved her. The lines in his face would ease then, just a little, as he realized that she spoke the truth.

It didn't happen. His mouth twisted in frustration and he raised a clenched fist over his head. For one frightening moment, Nora feared that he was actually going to strike out at her.

Instead, he waved the clenched fist in the air above her head. "If I find out that you've lied to me," he shouted, his face reddening with anger, "if I do, so help me . . ." Leaving the threat unfinished, he turned on his heel and ran down the steps, to his car.

But instead of getting in and driving away, he flung the back door open, reached in and scooped up something, and then turned back toward Nora.

His arms were filled with stuffed, crocheted animals.

Nora hadn't moved from her spot in the sun-drenched foyer. She recognized the toys in Professor Donner's arms. There was Bounce the kangaroo, his fur worn from years of hugging, and Harry the hippo. And hanging over the white sleeve by her leg was Lucy the llama, her glassy blue eyes staring up at Nora as if to say, "What is going on here?" All were hand-made by Nora's mother, physical therapy designed to battle her bouts of depression, and presented to Mindy many years later out of Nora's wish that they be enjoyed by another young child as much as she had enjoyed them.

While Nora watched in dismay, Professor Donner angrily flung the toys to the floor of the porch, shouting, "I don't want these things in my house! Is that how you got her to go with you? By offering her another one of these?"

"I . . . I didn't . . ." Nora stammered, not sure if she was protesting her innocence to the professor, or to the collection of stuffed animals lying at her feet.

A car Nora recognized as belonging to Fitz pulled up the long, gravel driveway. When it came to a halt in front of the house, Sabra, Amy, Lucas, and Fitz spilled out and ran up the porch steps.

Fitz glanced from Professor Donner's pur-pled, angry face to Nora's white, stricken expression and in two purposeful strides was at the professor's side, gently taking his arm.

"Hey, man, take it easy, okay?" he said quietly. "Nora hasn't done anything. It's just gossip, Professor, not worth two cents. You've got a wrong number here, and if you were thinking straight, you'd know that. Not that we blame you, of course," he added hastily. "But Nora isn't involved in Mindy's disappearance, okay?"

At least Fitz believed she was innocent.

Professor Donner, the fight apparently gone out of him, allowed Fitz to lead him from the house to his car. But Fitz wouldn't let him drive, taking him instead around to the passenger's side before returning to the driver's seat himself.

"He'll drive Donner back to his house," Lucas assured Nora. "And while he's doing that, I think maybe you should sit down." He led her into the foyer and pushed a chair at her. "Here, sit!"

Nora sat, in the brown wicker chair Mrs. Coates kept beside the telephone table. Her legs shook. She had to cross them to keep them still. Even then, the chair jiggled slightly in response to her involuntary body movements.

"Professor Donner can't believe that I would do such an awful thing," she said softly, staring at the open front door. "He can't really believe that."

"He doesn't," Lucas said emphatically. "The poor guy doesn't know what he's doing, that's all. He's half out of his mind with worry. Just forget it, Nora."

Nora shuddered. Forget it? As if that were possible. No matter what happened now, she knew the professor's shouted accusations, his pleas for help, would ring in her ears for a long time to come. No one had ever accused her of doing anything so horrible. The only accusation her aunt, with whom she lived following her father's death, had thrown at her was, "Nora, you're just like your mother. Much too emotional. If you're not careful, you'll end up just like her." That had been terrifying because her mother had died in the same psychiatric facility that she'd repeatedly been admitted to throughout Nora's childhood and adolescence.

"I'm not anything like my mother!" Nora had shouted defiantly in response to her aunt's chilly, dire prediction. But she had shouted because she was terrified that her aunt was right. Her mother had suffered from migraines, too, and often had memory lapses. Sometimes she hadn't even seemed to know who Nora was. She would look up from her crocheting or the book she was reading, see Nora sitting across the room doing her homework, and say in her light, gentle voice, "Nellie? Nellie, is that you?"

Nellie was Nora's grandmother's name.

Nora had memory lapses herself, and they terrified her. There seemed to be huge gaps in her childhood memories, extended periods of time when she was very young that were nothing more than a giant black void, as devoid of light as Nightmare Hall's vast, shadowed cellar. She couldn't remember a single Christmas or birthday before she was six, had no memory of entering kindergarten, could recall no favorite toys beyond the crocheted animals, and couldn't envision her grandparents' faces or even remember what their houses had looked like, although she knew she had visited them each time her mother was hospitalized.

Her friends in high school all seemed to know much more about their childhoods than Nora. That had scared her. Shouldn't she remember, too?

So when her aunt said, "You're just like your mother," it had terrified Nora. Only once had she herself ever been hospitalized. Briefly, but still . . .

The psychiatrist who treated her had said drily, "Well, of course your aunt thinks you're overemotional. For one thing, you're fifteen, and for another, your aunt is a stranger to her own emotions, let alone anyone else's. Don't judge yourself by her standards." She'd laughed. "That could really make you nuts."

The doctor's attitude had helped a lot. But her brief stay in the hospital hadn't allowed Nora to retrieve any childhood memories.

In spite of the fact that her aunt's accusation had eventually sent Nora into the hospital, it still didn't seem as terrible as the accusation Professor Donner had hurled at her. Taking Mindy, hiding her somewhere? Never, never!

Unless . . . could you do something like that, and then forget that you'd done it? The way she'd forgotten her childhood?

Her mother could have. Incidents resulting from her mother's terrible illness came flooding back in a dark rush. Nora coming home from school one hot, stifling day in early June to find the furnace going full-blast, the house dangerously suffocating, her mother huddled on the couch wrapped in blankets, insisting that this was the coldest December yet and wanting to know if Nora and her father had had any luck finding the perfect Christmas tree.

Coming home to a completely bare bedroom after playing at a friend's house on an autumn Saturday morning when she was eight. Her mother had donated all of Nora's bedroom furniture to a charitable organization. The truck was just pulling out of the driveway as Nora came up the sidewalk. Her mother had insisted that she had ordered all new furniture. "It's beautiful, Nora, with a canopy bed and book-cases and a triple dresser. You're going to love it."

But the furniture never arrived, because it had never been ordered. Nora had to sleep on the living room couch for two nights, until her father, in what Nora thought must have been a truly humiliating confrontation, had re-trieved her furniture.

The worst incident had been the baby stroller. On what Nora and her father had mis-takenly thought was one of her mother's "good days," the family had been enjoying an unac-customed outing to buy a new pair of sneakers for Nora. While she was trying them on, her mother had slipped out of the store and walked over to a woman standing beside a baby stroller that held a sleeping toddler. The woman, deep in conversation with a friend, didn't even notice as Margaret Mulgrew walked casually away, pushing the baby stroller, the baby still in it.

The ensuing commotion when the friend saw what was happening brought Nora and her fa-ther racing out of the store.

The following day, Nora's mother had returned once again to the hospital. This time, her stay had lasted a year.

If my mother, Nora thought, sick at heart, could do all of those things, and Aunt Colleen, her own sister, thinks I'm like her, how can I be so sure I didn't really take Mindy?

The question, one for which she had no answer, made her ill.

Chapter 10

"I tried to run away, of course. When I got older. But not when I first got there. I believed the woman when she told me I wasn't wanted back at the house in the country. So where could I run to? Even if I hadn't been only five years old, even if the house hadn't been out in the middle of nowhere like it was, there wasn't any place to run to.

"What did I know about police and other authorities like social workers, ready and willing to help me? I didn't even know that I'd been kidnapped, so how could I know what to do about it? There was no phone in the cabin, only a shortwave radio that I didn't know how to work. When I was older, she sent me out of the room whenever she used that radio, usually when a storm was due and she wanted the details. I knew she was afraid I'd learn to work the thing, but I didn't know why she was afraid.

Couldn't figure out who she was afraid I'd contact. By that time, when I was eight and nine and ten, I'd given up thinking about my other family. I would never have called them. Because I believed they didn't want me."

"Here, try these cookies. I have to go out again in a little while, and I don't want you to be hungry. You won't be able to sleep if you're hungry. I went to bed hungry lots of times, and I never could sleep. Here's some milk, too. Drink it up now. It's good for you."

"I'd already started kindergarten when I was taken, so I knew about school. I knew that I'd liked it, a lot. I already knew how to read. My mother taught me when I was four. I missed that so much, my mother sitting on my bed with me, her reading to me from Winnie-the-Pooh, *then me taking a turn reading to her. All the books the woman had in the cabin were old and smelled musty and were for grown-ups. When I started crying a lot, saying I wanted to go to school, she went into town in the truck and brought back a bunch of kids' books from the public library. I wanted to go there, too, but she said children weren't allowed in town. She said there was an ordinance against it because children were noisy and*

messy and caused trouble. I was five. I believed her. For a while, anyway.

"The books helped. As long as she kept bringing me books, I didn't whine about not going to school. But when the weather got bad and she couldn't get the truck out of the snowdrifts to go into town, I must have driven her crazy, nagging and whining because I was so bored I thought I was going to jump right out of my skin. There was nothing do in that stupid cabin! She taught me to play checkers and all kinds of card games, but when I started winning all the time, we quit playing. And she taught me to cook on that old, black iron stove. I wasn't really interested, but it took up some time, so it was better than nothing. And then after a while, I figured as soon as I could, I would get away from there and live by myself, so I'd need to know how to cook, anyway.

"The only things I knew about the outside world, I learned from magazines and books and television. So I knew there were other people out there, living a different kind of life. Not like mine at all. And I wanted that kind of life. The nicer kind, with a nice house and people around. The girls I read about in teen novels went to parties and did cheerleading and played musical instruments. They were pretty and popular and always dated the cutest boys. I hadn't seen a boy since I was five years old. I remembered him, too. His name was Justin Langley, and he was taller than anyone else in kindergarten. He had red hair and blue eyes and he used to kick my chair whenever he walked by, just to make me mad.

"I wondered if Justin ever thought about me, if he ever wondered why my parents had given me away. I wondered if he knew my sibling, if they were friends, if they ever talked about me.

"Could someone really talk about a sibling who had been given away by its parents? What would they say? How would they phrase it? 'Well, I had this brother or sister once upon a time, but it was a nuisance so my parents got rid of it and now I have the whole house to myself'?

"No, no one would ever say that because people would think they were weird.

"I guessed that no one ever talked about me.

"That was how I grew up. In a tiny cabin in the woods, miles from anything and anyone, my only companion a strange woman who needed very little in the way of entertainment

or socializing or money or comforts, and didn't
think that I should need those things, either.

"So you can complain all you want about
missing your daddy and Mary and that stupid
Norrie, but it's not so bad here, is it? At least
it's summer, and warm out. Now I have to go
out for a while, so you curl up there, nice and
cozy, and sleep. I'll be back in a little while.
Sleep tight. I'll be back soon, I promise."

Chapter 11

When Fitz returned, Nora was still seated in the wicker chair, but her legs had stopped shaking.

Fitz walked over to place a comforting hand on her shoulder. "He didn't mean it," he said of Professor Donner. "He's out of his skull with worry. He knows you didn't do it. Just not thinking clearly, that's all."

"He meant it," Nora said darkly, and would have added more bitter words if Jonah Reardon, in jeans and a deep-blue T-shirt, hadn't appeared in the doorway just then.

Nora didn't recognize him at first. No uniform, no cap, his brown, wavy hair blowing slightly in the morning breeze. He seemed taller than she'd first thought, and well-muscled in the T-shirt.

Taken by surprise, she said bluntly, "What are you doing here?" Realizing how rude that sounded, she added quickly, "I mean, you must be off-duty, or you'd be in uniform. So if you're off-duty," standing up, grateful that her legs were willing now to support her, "what are you doing here?"

"Can I come in?" He smiled. "Even without my uniform?"

"Sure," Amy said enthusiastically, "come on in. Nora here has had a horrible experience. Maybe you can help us cheer her up."

Nora shot her an annoyed glance. Amy didn't live at Nightingale Hall. She had no business inviting people inside. What if Nora didn't *want* Reardon in the house?

But she *did*, so the annoyance dissipated as quickly as it had come. Maybe he could tell her what to do, how to yank herself out of this horrible nightmare. He was a police officer, after all. Shouldn't he have some answers for her?

A second thought occurred to her then as Reardon walked over to her. A policeman wouldn't be given any time off while a small child was still missing. Could the fact that this one was out of uniform mean that Mindy had been found and was now safe at home? Was the search over?

Nora's heart began to pound with hope.

Which died a quick death when Reardon read the expression in her eyes and shook his head. "Nothing yet. I'm sorry." He let that sink in, his dark eyes filled with regret. Then he glanced at Amy and asked, "What did you mean about Nora having a bad experience? What happened?"

"I can speak for myself," Nora said tartly, disappointment washing over her. She told him about the visit from Professor Donner.

"Sorry," was his comment. "Must have been pretty ugly." He bent to pick up Harry the hippo. "These are the toys you gave the Donner girl?"

Nora nodded. "They were mine when I was little. My mother made them for me."

Reardon examined the stuffed hippo, turning it over repeatedly in his hands. He frowned. "These the only ones like this on campus?"

"I guess so. I mean, they're handmade. Not sold in stores. Unless other mothers make them for their kids, too." That didn't seem likely. Besides, how many college freshmen brought so many stuffed toys to campus? "Why?"

"Because I could swear I've seen one just like this before." Reardon held the hippo out in front of him. "Not this particular one. Not a hippo. It was . . ." he thought for a minute . . . "I think it was a bear. Big and round and dark brown. But it looked old, like this one, and it was made the same way."

"Well, it wasn't one of mine," Nora said flatly. "I never had a bear." They had moved several times when she was young. Maybe her father had believed that a new house was the key to her mother's peace of mind. It wasn't. During each move at least one member of her stuffed animal collection had been lost. But those missing creatures would hardly be turning up here on the campus of Salem University, miles from where she'd lived and so many years later. "I guess other people crochet stuffed animals, too."

While Reardon remained lost in concentration, Fitz astounded Nora by suggesting a short canoe ride on the river behind campus that afternoon.

She was incredulous. "A boat ride? Now? With Mindy still missing, and half the world thinking I took her? You expect me to casually float down the river in a boat as if I were Cleopatra on the Nile? God, Fitz, how can you be so insensitive?"

"*We* don't think you had anything to do with the kidnapping," Sabra said in an offended voice while Fitz flushed in anger. "We have some time before we have to rejoin the searchers. And I *don't* see what good it's going to do you to sit around the house alone and answer creepy phone calls."

"She won't be alone," Reardon interjected. "I'll be here. You guys go ahead. I have some details to go over with Nora, anyway."

"I thought you were off-duty," Lucas said. Nora thought she heard a note of resentment in his voice. But that made no sense. Why would Lucas care if Reardon stayed here with Nora? "Shouldn't you be out looking for Mindy? How come you're not on duty, anyway?"

"Being off-duty doesn't mean I can't talk to Nora," Reardon answered pleasantly. "And there are many, many people looking for the little girl. My captain thought it might be a good idea for someone to hang out here. But not in uniform. The box of fingernail clippings and the shoe we found in Nora's room are a pretty strong indication that the kidnapper has access to this house. We don't want a uniformed cop hanging around, keeping him in hiding. We want him out in the open, where we can see him."

"You mean you're using Nora to set a trap

for him?" Lucas asked, his tone one of disapproval.

"We don't look at it that way. Remember, Nora was clobbered by that swing at the day care center, and someone tossed a pitchfork at her in the barn. We don't know why, but we're pretty sure it's connected to the kidnapping. So if we can snag him while we're making sure Nora doesn't become a target again, so much the better."

"It was only a toy pitchfork," Lucas pointed out.

"No, it wasn't," Sabra disagreed. "It was child-sized, but it wasn't a toy. It was a real gardening tool, and the tines were really sharp, right, Nora?"

Nora nodded absentmindedly, but she was thinking about Reardon's comments. He was here to keep an eye on her? For her safety, as he'd said? Or to make sure she didn't split? Or maybe he'd been sent here to pretend concern in the hope that she'd confide in him, tell him where she was keeping Mindy. Was that it?

Was she still under suspicion, or wasn't she?

His conscience apparently stirred by Nora's disapproval of the canoe ride idea, Fitz canceled the outing, suggesting instead that they "hang out" with Nora until it was time to rejoin the search.

She didn't really want them to stay, but telling herself there was at least safety in numbers, she gave in, inviting them upstairs to her room but extracting from all of them a promise not to discuss the kidnapping.

Lounging about on the floor in Nora's room, they talked instead about the small town of Twin Falls and how boring it must be to grow up there, with so little to do, and they talked about summer classes and which professors they'd liked, and about how beautiful campus was, and how different from high school they expected college life to be.

But then Amy forgot her earlier promise and said, "I liked Professor Donner's summer history class. It was fun. He's such a fascinating lecturer." Her expression turned grim. "I just can't imagine what it must be like, having someone in your family missing."

Sabra shot her a warning glance, which Amy either didn't see or chose to ignore. "I mean, not even knowing where the person you love is, or if they're okay. And Mindy's so little . . ."

Silence fell across the bright, sunny room. No one responded for several seconds. Then Lucas said, "Well, I was an only child. I loved it. Spoiled rotten, and loved every minute of it. But my mother hated to let me out of her sight for more than two minutes, she was so afraid something would happen to me. If she'd ever gone through what Donner's going through, she'd have been a total basket case. Can't even imagine it."

Another minute or so of somber silence followed before Fitz said, "I had a sister once, when I was really little. I don't remember her at all. She died when I was only three or four, not even sure which. There are pictures of her in the house, but they're not very good ones. My parents didn't tell me about her. Someone in the neighborhood did. When I asked my mother about it, she ended up lying on her bed crying for hours, so I never brought it up again. When it happened, when she died, my parents must have gone through what Donner's going through."

Sabra, sitting on the floor leaning against Nora's bed, her long legs tucked underneath her, uttered a short laugh. "Well, there are so many kids in my family, I'm not sure my parents would notice if one of us was missing."

Amy was shocked. "Sabra! That's a terrible thing to say. I'm sure it's not true."

Sabra laughed again. "You don't know anything about my family, Amy. Let's just say it would at least take my folks a while to figure out which one of us was gone. They have a hard time keeping track of all of us. Besides, my dad drinks. A lot. Doesn't always know if *he's* even in the right house." She didn't sound bitter or angry, but accepting. "You're right, though. If one of us *was* missing, I guess they'd both freak." Sabra turned toward Amy. "What about your folks? Are you from a big family?"

Amy shook short, bouncy curls. "Nope, not me, although I always thought it would be fun to have lots of brothers and sisters. I'm adopted. My mother told me when I was six or seven. She was afraid someone else would tell me. I didn't know what it meant, but she said it meant that I was really special, and that's why they picked me. But both my parents died before I graduated from high school."

"Did you move in with relatives then?" Nora asked, thinking of her aunt.

"Nope. I just sort of floated from friend to friend." Amy's voice was light, almost cheerful, but her blue eyes seemed to Nora suspiciously bright, as if she might be struggling with unshed tears. "Got kicked out of one place for leaving wet towels lying on the new bathroom tile, something about mildew, and out of another because I wouldn't eat vegetables. My friend's mother thought that made me a bad influence on her younger kids. I felt kind of like a criminal." She laughed. "But I didn't argue. I left. Didn't much like the girl, anyway. Then I lived with one of my teachers, a nice, older lady, until I graduated. She helped me get my scholarship to Salem U."

Nora sat silently, listening attentively. She had thought of her own childhood as being bizarre, very different from the norm, mostly because of her mother's illness, the moving from house to house, and her own emotional problems. But Lucas had grown up an only child with an overprotective mother, Sabra's house was crowded and her father drank, Fitz's sister had died, and Amy had been just about homeless.

We're not all that different, Nora thought, surprised.

So where was the mythical perfect family she'd read about, dreamed about, wished for?

No sign of it in this room.

To Lucas, Amy said, "I thought you said you were going to become a pediatrician. The next Dr. Spock, you said. If you were an only child, how do you know if you even like children? You have to *like* kids to be a kids' doctor, Lucas."

Lucas laughed. "I didn't grow up alone on a desert island, Amy. I had friends. *They* were kids. Most of them had younger siblings. And don't forget, I was a kid, too. I know how a kid thinks and feels, right?"

Amy nodded dubiously. "I guess."

"Look," Jonah Reardon said then, "I need to talk to Nora alone. Police business. Would you guys mind splitting for a while?"

Lucas looked skeptical. "I don't think it's right to conduct police business when you're out of uniform."

"It's okay if it's important," Reardon said, sounding amused. "And this is, I promise."

"We have to get back to our search teams, anyway," Fitz said. "Maybe they've had some luck while we were gone."

But they all knew that wasn't likely. Nora had her radio on low, turned to the campus radio station, playing muted classical music in the background while they talked. They would have heard any bulletins about Mindy.

When the others had gone, Nora sat on her bed, leaned back against the wall, and looked at Reardon. "So, what's so important?"

"Oh, I did say it was important, didn't I? Well, it is, in a way." He moved to drag Nora's desk chair over near the bed, sitting in it backward, facing her. "I've been trying to remember where I saw that stuffed bear I told you about." He nodded toward the llama and the hippo lying in Nora's lap. She was holding the kangaroo in her hands, playing with its tail. "Like the ones you've got there."

"And have you remembered?"

"No. But it seems pretty weird to me that I saw another one of those somewhere else. Recently, too, I'm sure of that. Wish I could remember where."

"I don't see why. I told you, I never had a bear. So if you're thinking that the stuffed bear you saw could lead you to Mindy, it couldn't. I never gave her one, and I never saw one in her room. She would have told me if she had a bear exactly like the animals I'd given her."

Reardon didn't look convinced. "Still seems weird." Then he changed the subject by saying, "You're the only one who didn't talk about your family."

"Excuse me?" Nora shifted uncomfortably on the bed. Why did he have to bring that up? She'd been relieved that the others had left before anyone had asked about her family life. It wasn't something she talked about. Ever.

"Well, everyone else mentioned a little something about their backgrounds. But not you. I was just wondering why."

"There's nothing to tell, that's all," she said flippantly. "And are you asking out of interest, or because you're a cop?"

He groaned. "You're not going to hold that against me, are you? That I'm a cop?" But his tone was serious as he added, "I'm asking as a friend, that's all. Sometimes you have this . . . this almost haunted look in your eyes. At first, I thought it was because of the little girl, but now I'm not so sure. I think you've had that look for a long time. And I'm wondering why."

Nora hesitated. He seemed sincere enough. But he wasn't really a friend. Not yet, anyway. "You weren't sent here to interrogate me? To find out anything you could that might incriminate me in Mindy's kidnapping?"

He laughed a little when she said "incriminate." But he was perfectly serious again when he said, "I know I don't know you as well as those friends of yours do. But I can tell you for a fact that of all of us who were just sitting in this room, no one believes more strongly than I do that you're completely innocent. I don't believe you had anything to do with the Donner girl's kidnapping."

Nora didn't ask him *how* he knew. It didn't seem important. It was enough that he knew.

So she told him about her life. What she could remember of it. "And I think you should know," she finished, "because you're going to find out anyway, since I'm sure your police department is doing a background check on everyone who works at the center, that I was in a hospital for a while when I was fifteen. A psychiatric hospital. One my mother had been in many times before me, actually." She lifted her chin defiantly. "I wasn't there very long, and they said it was because both my parents had died so close together, so I had grief counseling and then I left. But some of the medication they gave me erased a lot of my memory from early childhood." She shrugged. "Not that I had that much to begin with. Never could remember anything that happened before my sixth birthday. Anyway," she concluded, her voice sinking despondently, "I thought everything was going to be fine when I came here. I thought *I* was fine. Coming here, getting away from my aunt, starting over. But now . . ."

Jonah Reardon reached out and took one of Nora's hands and held it gently. "You *are* fine," he said, his voice firm. "You didn't take that little girl. There's not a chance in hell that you're involved."

Grateful for the support, Nora said softly,

"Thanks." She withdrew her hand and sank back against the wall again. Her head was beginning to throb, so she closed her eyes.

They flew open a moment later at the sound of a voice calling her name.

But the voice wasn't Reardon's. He was still sitting there, facing her, but he wasn't speaking. So it wasn't his voice that Nora heard.

It was Mindy's.

Chapter 12

At the sound of the childish whimpering of her name, Nora bolted upright on her bed, clutching the stuffed animals to her chest.

Reardon's head whipped around, his eyes searching the room for the source of the sound.

It came again, louder and clearer this time. *"Nor-rie! Norrie, where are you?"*

Reardon jumped to his feet, sending the chair reeling backward. It toppled and fell, lying on the floor on its back like a wounded animal. "It's her, isn't it?" he asked, his eyes still scanning the room. "It's the little girl."

Nora, her eyes wide with shock, nodded silently.

"Where's it coming from?" Reardon moved swiftly to the closet, yanked the door open, scrutinized the contents.

"Nor-rie! Come get me, Norrie! I want to go home. I want my daddy."

While Nora watched, breathless, Reardon strode to the door of the room, opened it, stepped out into the hall, glancing first to his left, then to his right. When he stepped back inside, the childish voice seemed to fill the air. It was as clear and distinct as if Mindy Donner were standing in the center of the room.

"Nor-rie! Why don't you hurry to get me, Norrie? I've been waiting and waiting and waiting!"

Reardon turned to Nora, his face white, and said in a pained voice, "She's not here, is she? I couldn't have been that wrong about you."

Although she couldn't blame him, since the sound of Mindy's soft, sweet voice seemed to be wrapping itself around them, clinging, coaxing, impossible to ignore, Nora was filled with fury.

She jumped to her feet, her eyes blazing. "You *said* you knew I didn't take her!" she shouted. "You *said* you knew, more than anyone, that I wasn't involved!"

"And I *meant* it!" he shouted in return. "But . . . but I *hear* her, Nora. I hear her in this house. So do you."

"She isn't *here!*" Nora ran to the closet, flung the door open again, held it open as wide as it would go. "Look!" she commanded, "look in here, in this closet. Is she here? No, she is *not!*" She ran to the bed, bent to lift the dust ruffle, pointed underneath. "Here, look under here, is she there? Is Mindy under there, is that where I've been hiding her? No, she's not there, either, is she?"

While Reardon stood, stricken mute, in the center of the room, Nora dashed wildly from bed to desk to dresser, loudly defying him to find the missing child among her things. She ripped the desk drawers free, emptying their contents onto the floor, then ran to do the same with her dresser drawers, crying out the whole time, "Is she here? Is she? Do you see her? Do you, Reardon? Do you see Mindy anywhere in this room?"

He stopped her on her way to the dresser. In order to check her wild flight around the room, he had to step directly in her path and take hold of her upper arms. "Stop it, Nora!" he ordered, his voice steely. "Stop it right now! Of course the little girl isn't here. I'm sorry. I really am sorry. Hearing that voice, so close at hand, rattled me. I apologize. I meant what I said before. You didn't take her. I know you don't have her."

But she had begun to think that he wasn't like everyone else, hadn't she? Wasn't that why she had told him about her life? Because she'd begun to think he was different.

It hurt to know that he wasn't *that* different.

So instead of doing what she wanted to do, which was to collapse against his sturdy, solid chest, she jerked away from him, out of his grasp, and tilted her head angrily up at him. "Okay, so she's not in this room. But she could be anywhere in the house. Isn't that what you're thinking? And since I'm the only occupant of this house, except for the housemother, who I'm sure you'll agree probably isn't into kidnapping small children, doesn't that make *me* the prime suspect? Still?"

"Nora, calm down," Reardon warned. "I didn't mean . . ."

"Yes, you *did!*" Nora whirled then, and ran from the room. In the hall, she raced from door to door, throwing each door open and calling out Mindy's name in a shrill, fever-pitched voice.

When Reardon appeared in the hall behind her, Nora paused only for a second to shoot him a wild, defiant glance before resuming her mad rush from door to door. "Here!" she called out to him as she threw another door open, "maybe she's in here! Maybe this is where I've been hiding her all this time. You really should check it out, officer."

He stayed where he was, at the far end of the hall, a mixture of irritation and helplessness on his strong, handsome face.

"Well? Aren't you going to check it out? Dereliction of duty, if you ask me," Nora taunted, standing in the doorway of the room she had just opened. "What kind of cop are you, anyway?" Her face was red and flushed, her hair flying around her face, and she regarded him stonily with cold eyes that shone dangerously.

"Nor-rie! Help me, Norrie! I keep waiting, and you don't come. Where are you?"

Nora clapped her hands over her ears. "No! No, no more, *no!*" She shook her head from side to side, squeezing her hands against her ears as hard as she could.

Reardon reached her side, grabbed her, folded her against his chest. This time, Nora didn't resist. "Make it stop," she murmured into his T-shirt, "please, make it stop."

"It's not her," he said with authority. "It's not her. It's a trick. Someone mimicking a child's voice, that's all it is." Reardon glanced around the hallway, then up at the yellowed ceiling overhead. "The question is, where is it coming from?"

"Everywhere," Nora said softly, her voice muffled by his chest. "It's coming from everywhere!" She lifted her head then, looked up at him. "You really don't think it's Mindy? You're not just saying that because I freaked?"

"I should have noticed right off," he said apologetically. "But I've never heard the little girl speak, and it did sound like a kid at first. But listen, Nora. Listen to it carefully."

She still had her hands over her ears, but she could hear his words clearly. "No!" she cried stubbornly, pressing her hands more tightly against her ears. "I *won't* listen! It's horrible. I just want it to stop."

Reardon tugged at her hands, pulled them away from her ears, held them in his. "It isn't Mindy," he insisted. "Just listen, okay?"

"Nor-rie! I wanta see my daddy! Come get me!"

And this time, Nora heard what she hadn't heard before. She heard in the child's voice the same sinister, taunting tone of the voice in the barn, that disembodied voice that had sent the small but very sharp pitchfork flying at her from the loft.

"It's not Mindy," she breathed, her body sagging backward, against the wall, her eyes closing in relief. "You're right. It's not her. It's the other one."

"The other one?"

"It's the voice from the barn." Nora opened her eyes. "The barn you searched. I know you didn't find anything, but he *was* there." She shrugged her shoulders. "And now he's here." Her face was very pale, her eyes wide with fear.

"I don't *think* so. I don't think he's in the house. I think it's a recording."

"A recording?"

"Yeah. A tape. It sounds tinny. Our mimicking friend made a tape and probably used some kind of remote to turn it on. That way, there's no chance of him being caught when we hear the voice and go searching. He's already gone."

"He's not here?"

"Nope. I'll have to call this in, though. We need to find that tape and whatever kind of electronic equipment he's using. Might give us a clue."

"You do think it's the kidnapper doing all of this? Not just someone who's mad at me because they think I took Mindy?"

"Yep. I could be wrong, but that's what I

think. Wish I knew how the two things are connected, but I don't. Maybe it's just as simple as the fact that you were close to the child."

"*Am*," Nora said tremulously, "*am* close to the child. Please don't talk about Mindy in the past tense."

"Sorry."

The voice stopped then, as abruptly as it had begun. There was something about the sudden silence filling the hall that told Nora it was over. For now.

"C'mon," Reardon urged, taking her hand. "I'll call the station, we'll get some people out here to search, and this time it won't be just your room. I'm pretty sure that the captain will agree that this entire house, and the grounds, the barn, and the garage should all be searched. He'll have to drag a couple of men off the other search party, but they hadn't been having much luck on campus, anyway. Maybe they'll actually find something here."

While he made the phone call from Nora's room, she sat at the window, holding all of her stuffed animals for comfort, fighting to do two things: erase the taunting voice from her mind, and then, when that effort failed, concentrate instead on identifying it.

It had to be someone who not only knew Mindy well, but knew Nora, too. Knew where she lived, knew of her connection to Mindy, *and* knew when she was home and when she wasn't.

Nora drew in her breath sharply, her eyes darting to and fro in the room. Was someone watching her? Watching the house? If there really *was* a recording device, as Reardon suspected, wouldn't someone have had to be spying on the house to know when to play the tape?

Maybe they just played it at random, figuring sooner or later, she'd hear it.

Did they have to be inside the house to send the fake child's voice echoing through the halls?

"No," Reardon answered when he'd hung up the phone and Nora asked him the question, "not necessarily. With all the electronic equipment available today, he could probably be as far away as campus while we're here listening to his handiwork. A device planted here, a remote control in his hands, the push of a button, and we're listening to his Top-40. Simple. And very effective."

Nora shuddered. "I don't think he's that far away. I think he's much closer than campus. I can *feel* that someone's around. I think he's watching the house."

"Well, if he is, we'll find him. The captain is sending two officers to help search the place. Ditto the barn and garage. If he's here, we'll find him."

Nora sat in her room, the door locked upon Reardon's instructions, and waited. She could hear heavy feet tramping up and down stairs, padding across carpeting or tile, could hear doors opening and closing, drawers being slammed shut, deep, authoritative voices calling back and forth.

They won't find anything, she told herself angrily, aimlessly stroking Harry the hippo's fat nose. He's too clever. And then maybe Reardon's captain won't believe it was a recording. Maybe he and the other police officers will think it was Mindy's voice all along and that while they were busy searching for a recording device, I sneaked out of the house and spirited Mindy off to some other hiding place.

She heard them leaving the house, their footsteps on the damp ground echoing up into her open window. They went straight to the barn, their voices drifting around to the rear of the house. After a while, they returned to Nora's side of the house and moved to the garage and its upstairs apartment.

When she heard footsteps leaving the garage and heading back toward the house, she jumped up from the window seat, her arms still filled with stuffed animals, and hurried from the room, too anxious to learn what they might have discovered to wait until they arrived at her door.

Bright sunshine flooding in through the stained-glass half-moon window above the front door nearly blinded her as she reached the top of the stairs. She had to raise one hand to shield her eyes from the brilliant golden glow as she ran down the steps.

She was midway down the wide, curving staircase when she heard the voice. But this time it wasn't mimicking Mindy. This time, it was the voice of a full-grown adult that hissed down at Nora. *"Foolish girl, shielding your eyes like that. Don't you know you should keep your eyes wide open at all times? You just never know what might happen if you can't see what's coming, do you?"*

Gasping, Nora turned around on the stairs to glance up fearfully. She saw above her a figure so completely bathed in the streaming rays of sunshine that it was made indiscernible by the lemon-yellow garishness of the light.

As Nora turned to look up, her left heel, already on its way down to the next step, hit something. She knew instantly that it wasn't the solid, unyielding wood of the stair step that she'd been anticipating. Because the object moved beneath her foot. *Rolled* beneath her foot.

"And stay away from that cop or you'll be sorry!" the voice, hidden within the protective curtain of bright yellow light, hissed.

Nora's left foot began to roll backward.

The stairs at Nightingale Hall were old, and not very deep from front to back. There was little room on any step for maneuvering.

Nora tried. As her left foot sped backward without her consent, she fought hard to save herself. The stuffed animals flew out of her arms as she reached out to clutch at the stair railing. But the railing was no longer within reach. She struggled to maintain her balance, to stop the left foot's involuntary motion backward, but it was hopeless.

Her left leg rolled swiftly off the edge of the step, as if it wanted to separate itself from her, dealing Nora's equilibrium a final, fatal blow.

Although her arms flailed wildly in one last, desperate attempt to clutch the thick, wooden railing, her body was already toppling backward.

"*So long! See you next fall!*" she heard from above her.

Chapter 13

The woman I lived with knew nothing about teenagers. I had so many questions, but she wouldn't, or couldn't, answer them. I begged to be allowed to go into town with her. I wanted so much to see other people, see how they dressed and talked and what they did for fun. But she said I couldn't. That's all, I just couldn't. When I asked her why not, she said, "Never you mind."

I stole the truck once, to run away. I was thirteen. Didn't have the foggiest notion how to drive it, since she'd never let me go anywhere with her.

Still, I stole it, when she was napping late one winter afternoon. I just threw on the jacket she'd made me out of her old bathrobes, and pulled the cabin door open and sneaked out to the truck and climbed in. She always left the keys in the ignition, because there wasn't anyone way out there to steal it.

I turned the key and stomped down hard on all the pedals I could see. There were three, and I didn't know which was which, so I just slammed them all, really hard, and the truck made this horrendous, horrible noise and she came shooting out of that cabin like her hair was on fire. She wasn't all that young by then, but man, did she ever move fast!

I don't know who was more surprised when the truck moved, her or me, but all of a sudden, there I was, careening out of the yard and down the dirt path she took to town, trying to steer so I wouldn't hit the trees. I could just barely see over the steering wheel, had to sit up really straight and stretch my neck like crazy, and then my legs didn't want to reach, so I had to stretch them out, too, and that hurt.

She caught up with me, and jumped up on the running board. Probably one of the scariest moments of my life was seeing her face plastered to the window, her gray hair flying out around her, her eyes wild, using one fist to pound on the window while she held on to the door with her other hand.

I knew she wasn't going to give up, but I still

kept going, swerving this way and that because I really couldn't see very well, and it was getting dark very fast and I didn't know where the lights were, didn't know how to turn them on.

She was screaming at me through the window, I could hear her, screaming at me to stop, shouting that I couldn't leave her, I couldn't leave, what was I doing, where did I think I was going?

Away from her, that's where I was going. Away from her and that awful little cabin, away from the deadly loneliness and the crazy-making boredom and the weird, strange life that we led. I knew from magazines and books and television that it wasn't normal. Not even close. I wanted normal. I wanted what other people had. And to get that, I had to first get away from her.

I tried. I tried so hard, but I couldn't really drive the truck and it got dark so fast and then I couldn't see and she was still hanging on for dear life, pounding on the window and screaming at me to stop the truck, stop the truck right now!

I didn't stop it. A tree did. Didn't even see it coming at me out of the darkness, but suddenly, there it was, and I slammed into it or it slammed into me. She went flying off the running board and I was thrown into the steering wheel so hard, all the breath was knocked out of me.

I hadn't locked the door, because I didn't know you could, and the next thing I knew, there she was, dragging me out of the truck by my hair, and back into the cabin. Saying that I couldn't ever, ever leave her, not after all she'd done for me.

I never did ask her exactly what it was she had done for me.

I don't think I've ever been that scared since then. Her face smushed up against the window, me wanting so desperately to get away from there, from her, and then realizing that she wasn't going to let it happen, that she wasn't going to let me go . . . ever. Ever, ever, ever!

I stayed in bed for a week after that. She brought me soup, and I threw it at her. Finally, she said if I didn't open my mouth and eat something, she would hold my nose closed until I did open up, because if I didn't, I would die of starvation and she loved me and didn't want that.

Loved me? I didn't think so. That wasn't how my books talked about love. Keeping someone a prisoner, never letting them know other people or go to school or learn for themselves what life is really all about, I didn't think that was love. Maybe she thought it was, but I didn't. I knew better.

But I ate, finally. And after a while, I got out of bed and got dressed and did my chores.

I started reading again because I knew if I didn't, I really would lose my mind. She kept a real close eye on me after that. And she never left the keys in the truck again. I guess she kept them on her, because I never saw them lying around any place or hanging on a hook somewhere.

It was a long time before I tried running away again.

Chapter 14

Nora fell backward, and heavily, her body much too tense and rigid with fear to easily absorb a tumble down half a flight of bare wooden stairs. Her back hit first, her spine striking the hard edge of a step with a sharp, cracking sound. The force of that blow sent her head snapping backward. The still-tender spot on her skull from the collision with the dinosaur's pointed horns slammed into one of the lower steps.

She cried out in pain. The blow so stunned her that she scarcely felt her body continuing to tumble, heels over head, down the remaining steps.

She landed, semiconscious, at the bottom of the stairs. She lay stretched out, full-length, on the hardwood floor. It struck her dazed mind as odd that although she was aware of the cool, smooth floor beneath her body, her head seemed to be resting on something much softer. There had been no cracking sound when she'd landed, and she hadn't felt what should have been the severe impact of her head against wood.

Stunned and hurting, she lay perfectly still as running footsteps approached the front door. The police officers who had been searching outside must have heard her fall, heard her cry out, and were coming to help.

That was nice of them. Wasn't that nice of them? Now she wouldn't have to lie here all day with however many broken bones and maybe a fractured skull, and wonder if she was bleeding inside and would be dead by evening. Help was on its way. Nice.

Nora noticed, then, out of the corner of her eye that there was a little roller skate lying just inches from her aching head. A small, plastic, child's roller skate in bright primary colors of red and blue and yellow. It really was very small. Just about Mindy's size, Nora thought hazily with the part of her brain that was still functioning.

But, her brain pointed out, not so small that it couldn't almost kill someone whose left foot landed on it halfway down the middle of a steep staircase. Which, of course, anyone who might have planted the skate there would know. Anyone would know that.

So she knew that someone had put it there deliberately, and she knew that the skate had been meant for her.

That much, she was sure of.

"If you hadn't been carrying those stuffed animals," Jonah Reardon said as he knelt beside Nora, "you'd have split your skull open like a teacup." He pointed beneath her head. "You're lying on a stuffed hippopotamus."

"Harry? Harry saved my life?"

"Yep. Anything broken?"

Nora gingerly flexed arms and legs. "No, I don't think so."

One of the policemen moved toward the phone. "Ambulance," he said brusquely.

"No!" Nora pulled herself up on one elbow. "No ambulance, no hospital, no infirmary. I'm okay." But she winced in pain as she sat up all the way and her backbone reminded her of its collision with the stair step. To Reardon, she said, "There was someone here. Up there, at the top of the stairs. I couldn't see who it was. The sun blinded me. But he said I should watch where I was going, that I should stay away from you, and he left his calling card." She pointed to the brightly colored skate.

Jonah Reardon picked it up, held it in one hand. "This is what you tripped over?"

Nora nodded. "There aren't any little kids in this house. That roller skate doesn't belong to anyone here. *He* put it there. He knew I'd never even notice it. Of course, I might have if he hadn't called out to me." Nora shivered in revulsion. "He was *gloating*! He knew I was going to fall."

"Was it the same voice we heard earlier?"

"The same voice? Oh." Nora thought for a minute. "Well, he wasn't trying this time to sound like a small child, so I don't know. Maybe. It sounded . . . different. A kind of loud whisper. I couldn't even tell if it was male or female, and I'd never be able to identify it, if that's what you're asking."

While Reardon stayed with Nora, the other police officers once again searched the house. They returned to announce that any intruder had probably used the back staircase to make his getaway without being seen. "If he was at the top of the stairs like Miss Mulgrew says," the older officer said, "he could have heard us coming and run down the back stairs into the kitchen and out the back door while we were coming up the front steps."

Nora wasn't surprised that they hadn't found

her tormentor. She hadn't expected them to. But she was amazed that they weren't questioning her story about the voice at the top of the stairs. Their acceptance of it as truth was a real surprise.

"You sure you don't need a doctor?" the younger policeman asked her. "You look pretty shook to me. And that had to have been a real bad fall. Are you sure nothing's broken?"

"No, really, I'm fine. Thanks for asking, though." And although she wavered a little when she stood up, Nora soon regained her equilibrium. Except for a sharp, stinging sensation along her backbone that told her that she'd scraped at least one layer of skin off it, she felt reasonably okay. "It's not like I fell all the way from the top. I was halfway down the stairs when I hit the skate."

Remembering, Nora fell silent, realizing how lucky she had been. If *he* had arrived a moment or two sooner and given her a shove from the very top of the staircase, she wouldn't be standing on both feet now. She wouldn't be standing at all.

"What does he *want* from me?" she cried in frustration born of fear and confusion. "It can't be the kidnapper. He couldn't be running around watching me, torturing me. He has to stay with Mindy. Where would she be while he was at the day care center and the barn and at the top of the stairs in this house? She's only three years old. He couldn't be leaving her alone all this time."

"If he drugged her, he could," the older policeman said.

Nora gazed at him in alarm. "Drugged?"

"Wouldn't take much, a little kid like that. Kidnappers sometimes use sedatives to keep the kids quiet. Trouble is, they don't always know how much of a sedative is safe for a little kid. Sometimes . . ."

Reardon interrupted hastily. "He could just have her locked in a room somewhere that he knows she can't get out of. In an empty building somewhere, maybe. That way, he'd feel free to leave, knowing there wasn't anyone to hear her if she yelled."

"Yeah, could be."

But Nora saw the look that passed among the other two officers, and an icy finger touched her spine. They hadn't accepted Reardon's explanation. Which meant that they had a different one . . .

She didn't want to hear what that was.

Reardon called headquarters then, and got

an okay to stay at Nightingale Hall with Nora, and the other officers left.

The two sat on the bottom step, Nora cradling the stuffed animals in her arms. "You don't think she's dead, do you?" she couldn't help asking when they were alone.

He didn't hesitate even for a second. "Nope. Not for a minute. I think she's just fine. It's you I'm worried about."

Nora reached behind her to gently touch her bruised, scraped backbone. It hurt. "Me? I'm not the one who was kidnapped."

"No, but you're the one someone is making a target." Reardon swiveled on the step to face her. "Got any idea why?"

"I thought at first that it was someone who thinks I took Mindy. But I guess that doesn't make any sense. Because fracturing my skull with a swing or stabbing me with a pitchfork or sending me flying down a flight of stairs is a pretty stupid way to find out where I've hidden Mindy. I mean you were right about Harry here," gesturing with the stuffed hippo. "If I hadn't landed on him, I think I would have split my skull open." Nora forced a brief laugh. "Which means that I wouldn't even have been able to say my own name, never mind confessing where I had hidden my victim. Makes no sense at all. But if it's not someone trying to get a confession out of me, then I don't know *who* it could be."

"Anyone at the day care center jealous of you?"

The question surprised Nora. "Jealous? Why would someone be jealous of me?"

"Oh, gee, I don't know, Nora," Reardon said sarcastically. "Could it be because you're very easy to look at, the brain you almost splintered a few minutes ago seems to be a pretty good one, and you must be a pretty terrific person or that little three-year-old wouldn't have let you get so close to her. Three-year-olds are *very* fussy about who they associate with. I know because I have two nieces. One is three and one is five. The five-year-old is pretty friendly, but the little one spends a lot of time sizing people up before she gives them so much as a smile."

"If that's true," Nora said thoughtfully, ignoring the compliments paid her, "that just reinforces my theory that Mindy wouldn't have left her backyard with anyone she didn't know well."

Reardon sighed in mock exasperation. "I keep trying to talk about you, and the danger *you're* in here, and you keep changing the subject back to Mindy Donner. Look, I'm concerned about her, too, but she's got plenty of people concentrating on her. You, on the other hand, only have me, so far, so you ought to be paying attention to what I'm saying here. There isn't someone at the center who resented you, for whatever reason?"

Nora thought of Marjorie Dumas. There had been times at the center when Marjorie had become really incensed because Nora was occupying Mindy's time. She had once called Nora "selfish" in front of everyone, accusing her heatedly of "monopolizing" Mindy.

Childish. Childish and silly. But Marjorie had meant her words.

Nora debated silently. Should she tell Reardon about Marjorie's resentment? She didn't want to get an innocent person in trouble, especially now that she knew how horrible it was to be suspected of something you hadn't done.

But Mindy might have gone with Marjorie. She might have. She trusted everyone at the center, even Marjorie.

No. It wasn't Marjorie. She loved Mindy. She would never have taken the little girl away from her home and family.

But . . . if she thought that Nora *had*, she

might have decided to carry out her own brand of justice. She was certainly big enough and strong enough to heave a wooden swing, toss a pitchfork, and placing a child's roller skate on a stair for Nora to trip over might appeal to her bizarre sense of humor. She had once, after being reprimanded by Helen for tardiness, tacked a large, crude drawing of the director on a tree on the commons and tossed stones at it until the drawing was thoroughly pock-marked with small holes and dents. She had chuckled with relish the whole time she was pitching rocks at Helen's likeness.

Marjorie might very well chuckle at the sight of Nora Mulgrew taking a header down a flight of stairs. And she didn't strike Nora as being all that bright. It might not occur to her that if she caused too much damage, Nora would never be able to reveal where she had hidden Mindy.

"Well, there *is* this one girl," she began reluctantly, but before she could finish, the phone rang. Relieved, because she really loathed the idea of implicating someone without proof, Nora stood up and walked stiffly to the phone.

"Where are you hiding her?" a heated, angry voice demanded. "What have you done with that little girl? You're not going to go unpunished, I'll see to that!"

It wasn't the same voice that Nora had heard in the earlier phone call. This was deeper, rougher. More threatening, it seemed to her, although she realized that her current state of mind might be making it seem that way.

She clapped a hand over the mouthpiece. "It's a nasty phone call about Mindy," she told Reardon in a loud whisper. "I got one before, but this guy sounds really mad."

Reardon was at her side almost before she stopped speaking. He took the phone from her and barked into it, "This is Officer Jonah Reardon, Twin Falls Police Department. This line is being monitored. If you don't want to be charged with harassment, I suggest you hang up. And don't call this number again."

Nora heard the hasty click. She looked at Reardon with undisguised admiration. "Whoa! Not bad. Could you teach me how to get that don't-mess-around-with-me tone of voice? It's pretty impressive."

He didn't laugh. "How many calls like that have you had? And why didn't you report them? Or at least tell me?"

"This was only the second one." Nora replaced the telephone and returned to the stair step. "And why would I report it? The person on the phone was only saying what everyone else is thinking."

"Did he threaten you?" He didn't join her on the step, but leaned against the wooden railing, looking down at her.

"I guess so. He said I wouldn't go unpunished, or something like that." She shrugged. "Maybe that's why the roller skate was on the stair. A broken neck or back certainly seems like punishment to me."

Reardon shook his head in doubt. "If this guy who just called had put the skate there, he'd have been surprised that you were able to answer the phone. Was he?"

"I was the only one surprised," Nora answered grimly.

"Then it wasn't him. Someone else put the skate there. And this was just a crank call."

Nora wanted to believe him. If only because the thought of more than one person being violently angry with her was just too much. But the guy hadn't sounded all that harmless. And now he'd be doubly mad at her because a policeman had threatened him on her behalf.

The sun continued to stream in through the door window, but the air in the foyer was cool as the pair fell silent, lost in thought.

The sound of tires crunching on the gravel driveway brought their heads up. Car doors slammed, feet ran up the steps, the front door opened.

Amy stood there, her face alight. "They've found her!" she cried, a broad smile on her tanned, oval face. "They know where Mindy is!"

Chapter 15

When Amy shouted, "They've found her!" Nora forgot all about her fall down the stairs, the taunting voice, the roller skate. As she stood up, all of her thoughts went to Mindy.

"Found her? Where? Is she okay? She's not hurt, is she?"

"Don't know," Amy answered. "We were searching the area near the campus tower when Marjorie Dumas ran up and said the police had received a phone tip that the missing child was in a house on Fourth Street in Twin Falls. They're on their way there now."

Nora whirled, faced Reardon. "You can find out which house," she said urgently. "Call in on your radio and ask, okay? I want to go down there."

He shook his head. "No way. You're not going near that place. If the kidnapper's there, all hell could break loose. If he's the one targeting you, he could go for your throat the minute he sees you."

"I don't care. I want to be there when they find her. She'll be scared by all those cops. She'll need to see a friendly face."

"I'll go," Amy volunteered. "She knows me, Nora. And I was part of the search party, so no one will be surprised that I know where the house is. But you weren't. If you show up down there before the address is released to the public, everyone will think you knew all along where Mindy was. Because you put her there. Or helped someone else do it."

"Mindy will tell them it wasn't me."

"*If* she saw the kidnapper's face," Reardon said. "What if she didn't? Most kidnappers who don't intend to kill . . ." Seeing the look on her face, he cleared his throat and tried again. "Who intend to let their victims go eventually, disguise themselves so they can't be identified. He probably disguised his voice, too. Anyway, she's only three, Nora. How good can she be at distinguishing one voice from another?"

"He's right," Amy agreed, nodding.

Nora's heart sank. She had been counting on Mindy to clear her, when the little girl was found. Was Reardon right? Would Mindy not be able to say for certain that her captor hadn't been Nora Mulgrew?

She didn't think the police still considered her a suspect, not after everything that had happened. But the whole town and everyone on campus probably still did. If Mindy was alone in the house, with no sign of the kidnapper, Mindy's father would be bitterly disappointed that the criminal responsible for his daughter's disappearance hadn't been apprehended. So if Nora showed up on the scene, he might turn on her again, in front of a crowd of people.

She couldn't deal with that. Not now. She was still too shaky from the voice at the top of the stairs, and her fall.

"Okay," she said, sighing in defeat. "You're right. I'll stay here. But you call me the very second that Mindy is safe, Amy. Promise!"

"I promise."

Reardon pursed his lips in concentration. "You can't stay here alone," he said to Nora. "When is your housemother due back?"

"I'm not sure. Sometimes she spends Sunday with friends. She could be gone all day."

"You could go to the day care center," Amy suggested. "We're all meeting back there to celebrate. You could wait for us there."

Nora remembered the painful thwack of the swing against her temple, and winced. "I don't think so. Actually, I think I'm safer here right now than anywhere else." Turning to Reardon, she clarified, "The house and the barn and garage have all been searched, right? And you didn't find anything, did you?"

"No. No sign of anyone and no recording device, either. But I know it's here. I'm sure that's what it was." He moved to the telephone to call headquarters.

"Then I'll stay here," Nora told Amy. "I'll lock the doors and I'll wait for all of you here. If the kidnapper is caught at that house, you can pick me up on your way back to the day care center and I'll celebrate with you. This horrible nightmare will be over and I'll be able to relax like everyone else."

"And if he's not caught?" Amy asked quietly. "If he's not there, at the house with Mindy?"

"He *will* be," Reardon answered, replacing the telephone. "And even if he isn't, at least Nora's not a suspect anymore. Captain Dwyer says it's too obvious that someone is trying to implicate her. Exactly what I've been saying all along. And she's been attacked too many times. Don't know what that's all about, but it puts her out of the running as a suspect."

"Well, that's great!" Amy said heartily. "I'll spread the word. Not that any of us *ever* thought she was involved."

"Actually," Reardon said, his voice uneasy, "you can't do that, Amy. Dwyer says if the kidnapper isn't at the Fourth Street house, Nora is our best bet to catch the guy." He glanced apologetically at Nora. "Not that we'd ever let anything happen to you."

"Something already *did*," Nora said quietly. "Several somethings."

"My fault. I should have stayed with you while the other guys searched the property. And I'm not going to make the same mistake again. I'm staying here with you. Amy, you and the others go ahead, okay? Just call us and tell us what happened."

Nora heard the regret in his voice. Jonah Reardon was a cop. He'd been involved with the effort to find Mindy Donner from the beginning. He wanted to be there for the happy conclusion, and Nora didn't blame him. He *should* be there.

"Thanks, that's really nice of you," she told him. "But the truth is, I feel another migraine coming on." There was no migraine, but her head *did* hurt. Not such a big lie, and it was for a good reason, wasn't it? "Not only can you not do anything to help, but if you're here, moving around the house, making even the tiniest bit of noise, it'll make me scream. If you so much as turn on a faucet to get a drink, my head will feel like it's going to explode. An empty, totally silent house is the best treatment for a migraine. And like I said, there's no one here, nothing here to hurt me. You and the other officers made sure of that."

"I'm not going," he said stubbornly.

"Yeah, you are. I need you out of here." She could see by the expression on his face that he wasn't giving in. So she took a deep breath and added casually, "Anyway, it's not like it's done me so much good having you around in the past, right?"

Amy gasped, and Reardon's handsome face flushed scarlet. "You don't think I can hack it here?" he asked stiffly.

She couldn't back down now. He deserved to be at that house on Fourth Street when Mindy was found. Besides, it wasn't as if she was being noble or anything. They *had* searched the property. If she thought evil was lurking somewhere in the shadows, she'd never have urged him to go, not even if he begged.

"But . . ." Reardon began.

Nora waved a hand in dismissal. "Just go, okay? I'll be fine. All I need to do is go to bed. Amy, *call* me! The minute Mindy is safe. Migraine or no migraine, I want that phone call! Don't wait until you get back here to let me in on the good news."

Amy nodded. "I won't. You'll know a second after we know, I promise."

She left.

Reardon hesitated, then, when Nora gave no hint that she would rather have him stay, he moved toward the door. "Lock this!" he commanded sharply as he pulled it closed. He didn't look at Nora when he said it and she knew he was deeply hurt.

He'd get over it. Maybe he'd even thank her some day.

Maybe not.

She couldn't worry about that now. It would ruin her excitement over Mindy being found. As it was, she was going to have a hard time sitting still until that phone call came.

When she had locked the front door, Nora scooped up the stuffed animals scattered at the foot of the stairs. If the kidnapper was caught, Professor Donner would apologize to her for his accusations, and he'd let Mindy have her animals back again. In the meantime, they were in serious need of a bath. It was something to do, something to keep her busy until she heard the jangle of a telephone ringing.

Keeping busy would make the time go faster. She'd wash the animals out by hand and dry them on the clothesline near the barn, where the sun would dry them quickly. When she returned them to Mindy, they'd smell fresh and clean.

She was up to her elbows in suds, standing at the kitchen sink gazing out the window overlooking the sunny, wooded back yard, when a memory hit her that was so clear and vivid, it took her breath away.

A woman . . . tall, pretty, pale, curly hair like Nora's . . . her mother again . . . was standing at a kitchen sink just like this one, looking out a similar window into a somewhat larger, more level back lawn. She was crying. Crying hard, almost sobbing, not even bothering to wipe the tears from her face. Crying in what seemed to Nora like hopeless despair.

A small child stood at her side, tugging on her arm. "Mommy, mommy," the child whispered anxiously, "what's wrong? Why are you crying? Was I bad?"

"Nell," the woman sobbed, ignoring the child tugging on her arm, "oh, Nell, I miss you!"

The memory disappeared then, as if someone had switched off a television program Nora was watching.

She leaned against the sink, thoroughly shaken. The images had been so clear. She remembered different details. A stained-glass bird in brilliant blues and green had hung in the kitchen window, its colors made even more vibrant by the sun's rays. A red-checked apron tied around the woman's waist, over her jeans. A blue plastic dishpan sitting in the sink, overflowing with foamy suds. A heavy wooden playscape in the yard outside the window, the empty swings stirred gently by a light breeze.

None of it seemed familiar to Nora. Yet it hadn't been a dream. She was wide-awake. And although nothing else in the vision had seemed familiar, Nora was convinced the woman at the sink was her mother.

She realized then, why her mother had been crying. Nell was Nora's grandmother's name. The episode, if it really had happened, must have taken place shortly after they'd moved the first time, away from Nora's grandparents and the town where Margaret Mulgrew had grown up, had spent her entire life. It must have been hard for her, moving away from family and friends. How could Nora's father ever have thought such a move would help her mother?

She knew the crying couldn't have been caused by her grandmother's death, because her grandmother hadn't died until Nora was fifteen, and the child standing at her mother's side at the sink was very small. So it had to be simple homesickness that had made Nora's mother cry out her own mother's name with such sadness.

Later, they had moved back to that town so that Nora's grandparents could take care of her during her mother's bouts of illness.

But that move hadn't helped, either.

It wasn't that the sight of her mother crying at the kitchen sink was so shocking to Nora. It wasn't. On "bad days," her mother had often cried. But Nora had never before had such a vivid memory of one of those incidents.

She found it very upsetting. Whatever it was that had caused her mother's unhappiness, the child at her side had clearly thought it was *her* fault.

And her mother hadn't told her that it wasn't.

I do remember thinking her "bad days" were my fault, Nora reflected as she squeezed soap from the sodden crocheted animals, but I thought that came later, when I was ten or eleven. I don't remember thinking it when I was very small.

But then, she remembered so little of when she was very small.

Nora rinsed the animals thoroughly, squeezed the excess water from them, wrapped them in a heavy towel, and took the bundle outside into the hot, sunny afternoon.

But she opened the back door very slowly and didn't take one step outside until she had peered around her intently to make sure she was still alone.

She saw nothing, heard nothing, out of the ordinary. Only normal sounds. The birds chirping in the woods behind the barn, the distant hum of tires on the highway below the front of the house, a steady dripping sound from a hose attached to a faucet on the side of the barn. No threatening voice. No whoosh of a swing or a pitchfork flying at her.

Reardon and the other police officers had found nothing because there *was* nothing.

She was alone.

She opened the door all the way, and dripping towel in hand, hurried across the yard to the clothesline.

There were no clothespins on the line strung

between two T-shaped metal poles. Nora had been drying her own laundry in the industrial-sized machine housed behind white louvered doors in the kitchen. But she was afraid the foam rubber stuffing inside the toys would melt under the dryer's intense heat. Besides, they would smell much fresher if they were hung outside, even on such a hot day.

Finding no clothespins on the line made her anxious. She hadn't planned to be outside more than a minute or two. Amy could call at any moment, and the ring of the telephone might not be audible out here.

Where did Mrs. Coates keep the stupid clothespins?

Unwilling to risk missing a phone call that could make all the difference in her life, Nora refused to waste time hunting for clothespins. Instead, she affixed the animals to the line by twisting their tails or legs around the plastic-coated rope. If the wind didn't suddenly pick up, all four animals should remain in place until they were dry.

It was hot enough that they just might be dry by the time Mindy was brought safely home. Then Nora could take them to her, smelling fresh and sweet. Professor Donner would apologize, and maybe Mary would do the same, although that seemed unlikely. At least she couldn't possibly bar Nora from the house now. Not with Mindy safe at home and the person who had taken her safely behind bars.

What if the kidnapper wasn't there, at the house on Fourth Street when the police arrived?

The footsteps behind her, crackling on the hot, dry ground, appeared as suddenly as if an intruder had been dropped from the sky.

Nora's heart stopped.

She hadn't heard the footsteps coming up the grassy hill from the highway or crunching on the gravel driveway or clattering down the wooden steps from the garage apartment or hurrying out of the barn or climbing up the wooded hill behind the property. She had heard nothing. They were just suddenly there behind her, crunching purposely toward her.

What if the kidnapper was in the backyard at Nightingale Hall?

Her back still to the footsteps, her body at full alert, Nora called over her shoulder, "Jonah? Jonah Reardon? Is that you?"

But she knew that it wasn't.

"Didn't I tell you to stay away from that cop?" the voice she had heard at the top of the stairs as she had toppled backward whispered

now in her ear. *"I saw him here, just a little while ago. No uniform, but it was him, all right. You shouldn't ignore my warnings. That was very foolish of you."*

Nora had already begun to turn, but she was stopped in mid-spin and lifted off her feet by something smooth and strong wrapped around her neck and tugged backward.

The only sound she had time to make was a strangled, gasped, "No!"

Chapter 16

Nora's hands flew frantically to her throat, pulling, clawing at the slick rope around her neck. At the same time, she kicked wildly, struggling to get her feet back on the ground. But her captor was stronger, angrier, hauling her backward with determination, like someone dragging a sack of trash to the curb.

As she fought, Nora tried valiantly to scream, but the rope around her neck was too tight. It hurt, and the harder he tugged on it from behind, the harder it was for her to take a breath.

"I warned you, didn't I?" Muttering, low, hoarse muttering, behind her. *"More than once I warned you, and you wouldn't listen. You are so stubborn, so arrogant. I knew you were spoiled rotten. Someone should have taught you to pay attention when other people speak."*

The sun was still shining brightly directly overhead, the sky pale blue and cloudless. A bird sang somewhere in the woods, and a sudden gust of wind tore the petals off a dying rose beside the house. They flew past Nora as if to say, "See? We're free to go where we like, and you're not."

It was an oddly peaceful, tranquil scene that met Nora's eyes as she fought for her life.

Fighting, flailing desperately at the air with one arm while the other kept fingers at her throat struggling to loosen the rope that was strangling her, Nora memorized the scene before her eyes. If it was going to be the last thing she ever saw in her life, she wanted to hold onto it as long as she could. It was already rapidly fading from view as her lungs continued to be deprived of oxygen. Her dazed mind told her she only had a few seconds left to live.

Inside the house, the telephone rang. The shrill, insistent sound echoed out into the back yard, circling around the struggling pair like an alarm.

Nora's captor hadn't been expecting the sound, any more than Nora had. The sound startled him. He paused, just for a moment, and released his grip slightly on the rope.

She felt the pause, became aware of a slight easing of the tension on the rope around her neck. It couldn't last more than a second, she knew that. The sound was only a ringing telephone, after all, not a police car's siren.

No time to waste. Nora threw herself sideways, the rope still around her neck, knowing she was risking strangulation by jerking away so swiftly. Such a move could break her neck. But she wasn't passing up this one chance. Her hope was that the sudden pull on the rope when he least expected it would yank it from his hands. It was a weak, desperate hope, one she hadn't thought out clearly, and she knew even as she flung her body sideways that if the sudden move snapped her neck in two, she would die.

But if she didn't do something now, in this one single moment of distraction, she would die, anyway.

It worked. Her sudden, unexpected, vigorous movement ripped his end of the rope out of his hands, and then Nora was up on her feet again and running toward the house, knowing she couldn't be more than a step or two ahead of him.

She had never run so fast in her life.

The rope was still around her neck, but it had loosened slightly. Still, tiny spots of navy blue danced before her eyes and the pain in her chest hadn't eased. But if she could make it into the house, snatch up the phone before he caught up with her, and if Amy was still on the other end of the line, if she hadn't already hung up, there was hope. . . .

One hand still tugging at the painful rope digging into her flesh, Nora threw herself at the back door. It burst open under her weight and she fell onto the small back porch. Then she whirled quickly to drop the latch in place, surprised that she hadn't been grabbed from behind before she could do that. The old, flimsy screen door wouldn't keep anyone out, but she locked it, anyway.

Then, as both hands returned to her throat to further loosen the rope, Nora found herself staring out across the back lawn in confusion.

There was no one following her.

There was no one out there.

The sun was still shining, the sky still blue, the breeze still active, stirring the animals dripping from the clothesline. But there was no one racing after her, no one stumbling up the steps in a fury, no one trying to force the

screen door open to get at her, no one screaming at her in rage.

He was gone.

The front door was locked. He couldn't get
in that way. And there was no other door at
the back of the house. The only other entrance
was through the cellar. Those doors might be
unlocked, but the door from the cellar into the
kitchen was firmly locked. Nora had checked
it herself after Amy and Reardon left.

She threw the heavy, wooden back door shut
upon the screen and locked it.

He couldn't get in. If he was only playing
possum, hiding around a corner of the house,
biding his time before his next attack, he'd be
disappointed when he tried to enter the house.

Nora staggered into the kitchen and yanked
a sharp knife from a drawer. As carefully as
she could, she sawed at the thick rope around
her neck until it gave. She nicked the skin on
her neck twice, drawing blood, and sliced the
index finger on her left hand, but she didn't
care. What were a few minor cuts compared to
strangulation?

The rope fell to the floor. Nora leaned
against the sink, drawing huge, gulping mouth-
fuls of air. When the pain in her chest had

eased, she filled a glass with water and drank it slowly to soothe the raw ache in her throat. Then she sank into a kitchen chair and reached down to pick up the wicked noose that had almost taken her life.

She knew right away what it was. Not just a plain old rope. Of course not. There was a message here, just as there had been with the child's swing and the child's pitchfork and the child's roller skate.

A jump rope. The thing around her neck that had come so close to choking the life out of her was a child's jump rope. Red and white striped, thick but flexible.

A jump rope.

Nora sat at the table, her head aching, her throat sore, the little cuts on her neck stinging. Why hadn't he followed her into the house? He could have caught up with her easily. But he hadn't. He must have known there was no one else in the house, or he wouldn't have attacked her in the back yard in the first place. So if he knew the house was empty, why not follow her inside and finish her off? It wouldn't have taken long. No more than a few seconds.

But he'd run away instead.

Why?

He wasn't trying to kill you, came the answer. He never intended to kill you. Think about it. What are the chances that a wooden swing would take someone's life? Or a child's pitchfork? Why not a real pitchfork? There's one in the barn. He could have used that, right? And if he'd truly meant to kill you by placing a roller skate on the stairs, wouldn't he have stuck it on one of the top stairs instead of halfway down, where the chances of a fatal injury would be much smaller? He wasn't trying to kill you. He was just torturing you. That's all he meant to do. For *now* . . .

That seemed, in a way, almost scarier than the thought of dying. Because it was clear that he hadn't finished with her. There was more to come, she was frighteningly certain of that. That's *why* she was still alive.

But she was equally certain that when he had finished "punishing" her, he would finish her off. He wouldn't leave her alive to tell the tale.

It *did* have something to do with Mindy, she was sure of that, too. Every instrument used to "torture" her had been a child's thing. A swing, a youth-sized pitchfork, a child's roller skate, and now, a jump rope. That part of the message was clear.

But what was the other part? She hadn't kidnapped Mindy. Hadn't had anything to do with it. Shouldn't be punished for it when she was innocent.

Then . . . was there some other reason she was being attacked?

A familiar sound outside brought her to her feet. Tires on the driveway again. Feet approaching the house.

Eyes wide with apprehension, Nora ran to stand with her back against the kitchen sink, her hands at her mouth. Had he come back?

He wasn't driving, stupid, her brain said. If he had been, you'd have heard him pull up into the driveway when you were hanging those animals on the line. It's someone else.

It was. A second or two later, a sharp knocking sounded on the front door and Amy's voice called, "Nora? Nora, open the door! It's okay, it's us."

Her face alight with anticipation, Nora hurried down the hall to unlock the door and pull it open.

Amy and a now-uniformed Reardon stood on the porch.

Nora knew the minute she saw the expression on Amy's face. The light went out of her face and she sagged back against the door. "Oh, no," she breathed, "oh, no. They didn't find her, did they? She wasn't at the house on Fourth Street. She's still missing."

"Yes," Amy said, her voice heavy with regret. "She's still missing."

Chapter 17

I tried running away again twice after that first time.

The first time was in the dead of winter, the same time of year that I'd been taken. I never had any Christmas that year, you know. The woman wanted someone with her for the holidays, although she never had a tree or wrapped presents. She did bake some really icky-tasting cookies, I remember. They weren't sweet, like the sugar cookie Christmas trees and wreaths and snowmen I remembered.

I didn't take the truck the second time I ran away. I'd learned my lesson. I had no idea where anything was, not the town or a bus station or a train. But I thought I could follow the track she drove the truck on, and that would lead to something.

It was very cold that night, the kind of cold that gets down inside your bones. I knew I should wait for a better night, but I'd been patient so long already. And I couldn't stand the thought of spending another dark, gray Christmas in that cabin. I didn't know where I was going. It's not like I had a family to go back to. I hardly remembered them, and was sure they didn't want me. I believed that even if by some miracle I could locate them and showed up on their doorstep, they'd open the door, see me standing there, and look at me like I was a creature from another planet. Then they'd make me leave. Or maybe my sibling would open the door, stare at me, recognize who I was, and call the police to cart me away.

Something horrible would happen, I was sure of that. So I wasn't going to try and find them. Not ever. It was too late for that. Much too late. I'd been gone nine whole years.

And all that time, my sibling had been living in what I remembered as a big, beautiful house with kind, loving parents. I couldn't remember their faces, but I could remember being sung to and read to although more and more often I couldn't tell if those things were real memories or if I was creating lovely fantasies in my head.

All of those years, I'd had nothing. Nothing, that is, but misery. While the other child had

had everything. Everything! Everything that was supposed to be mine, too. Without ever having to share.

By that time, I knew the woman had lied about my parents giving me up willingly. I knew that wasn't true. But I also believed they hadn't tried very hard to find me. If they had, they would have succeeded, wouldn't they? And I was convinced that the reason they hadn't tried very hard, was the other child. If they hadn't had it, they might have moved heaven and earth in their efforts to find me. But they still had that child. Comforted by that thought, they had given up on me much too easily.

How happy that child must have been that it hadn't called out for help in time when I was carried into the woods. How it must have relished its lovely life, while I was suffering through mine.

That fall, long before the snow flew, I started fantasizing about one day finding my family, not to reunite with them, never that, for it was much too late, but to simply seek justice. It wasn't right that I'd had so much taken away from me. It wasn't right.

I had no idea where they were. But I was more determined to find them than they must have been to find me. I would succeed where they had failed. And then I would face them and say, "Look what you let happen to me."

Especially the child.

On that winter night when I was fourteen, I didn't know if I was going to begin my hunt that night or not. All I was certain of was I couldn't spend another horrible Christmas in that cold, grim cabin with that quiet, creepy old lady.

So, when she fell asleep in her chair after dinner as she did every night, I left the cabin.

The woods on both sides of the truck track were dark and deep, the trees bare, their limbs reaching out like bony fingers to clutch at me. I stayed well in the middle of the path. I had no idea how far town was, but I hoped the snow wouldn't begin falling until I'd reached civilization. It would be easy, in a blizzard, to become lost forever in these woods, and I didn't want to die that night. I had places to go, things to do, people to see. Revenge to seek . . .

But I'd only been walking for twenty minutes or so when my right foot slipped into a burrow in the snow and I broke my ankle trying to get my leg out.

I had to sit there on the ground, crying in bitter frustration, until the old lady came and got me, clucking her tongue and pretending all

I'd done was go out to play in the snow.

I fainted when she set my ankle.

She didn't have to worry about me trying it again anytime soon. She'd done a good job with the ankle, which is why I don't limp, but I couldn't walk on it for a long time.

I was fifteen before I tried again.

This time I waited until summer, and I did think seriously about taking the truck again. But it was on its last legs by then, and I was afraid I'd get only so far and then it would die and I'd be stranded. Besides, the woman still had the shortwave radio. If I took the truck, she'd notice too quickly that I was gone, and get on that radio and call the state police. Of course, she'd have had some explaining to do about who I was. No one in town knew she had anyone living with her.

So I would have taken the truck and let the police pick me up and then I would have told them who I really was, except for one thing. I no longer remembered who I really was. I couldn't remember my real name, first or last, and I didn't know the name of the town I'd lived in before the cabin in the woods. I tried and I tried, but it was all gone, so much so that sometimes I actually wondered if I'd dreamed the whole thing and the old lady really was the only mother I'd ever had.

No, I knew that wasn't true. She wasn't. She couldn't be. No way.

Besides, I had proof that I had once been someone else. And I planned to take that proof with me. It wouldn't mean anything to anyone except my family. A policeman wouldn't be impressed. But my parents, even my hated, treacherous sibling would know, when they saw it.

How did I expect to find my real family if I couldn't remember anything about them?

I don't know how I expected to do it. I only knew that I would.

I was all ready to go on that hot summer night. But this time I was going to wait until she was asleep for the night. She slept deeply, sometimes snoring so loudly that I couldn't sleep. If I left shortly after she fell asleep, I'd have hours of travel time in before she awoke at dawn the next morning.

While she took her evening nap, I packed a few sandwiches and a couple of apples from the six spindly trees out back. I didn't want to be weighted down with anything else. The only other thing I took was the single piece of proof that I hadn't been born to the old woman, that I had once been some other woman's child.

I waited until I was sure she was asleep. Then I tiptoed to the door and was just about to open it when I heard a really weird sound from the bedroom. A kind of gasp-sighing noise. There was something about it . . . I knew something was wrong even before I went in there and looked at her face and saw that she had died. Even before I checked and found that she wasn't breathing, I knew. I don't know how. I'd never seen anyone die before. I just knew.

Dead! Just like that. She wasn't even sick. And I hadn't thought she was that old.

But she hadn't had an easy life.

I didn't know what to do. No one knew about me. We didn't have a telephone and she had never taught me how to use the radio.

I decided I didn't owe her anything. If anything, it was the other way around. She owed me for the life she'd taken away from me. A good life. A happy life.

Sooner or later, someone from town would wonder where she was and come looking for her.

So I just left.

But before I did, I searched the cabin thoroughly. I needed money. Couldn't get very far without money, and I was only fifteen, not old enough to get a real job.

I did find some money. A packet of bills rolled up and tied with a rubber band, hidden in a cookie jar in the kitchen. It wasn't a ton of money, but it was better than nothing.

And I found something else in my search. Newspaper articles, under a loose floorboard in the bedroom. I'd never seen a newspaper in the cabin, so she had to have bought the papers in town, read them in the truck, and then sneaked them into the house and buried them under the loose board when I wasn't around.

I knew why she'd kept them. They were about me. About my kidnapping. Stories about how I'd been taken, and how my parents were "distraught" with grief and worry. "Distraught"? That made it sound like they'd cared.

If they'd cared so much, why had they quit looking for me?

When I had read all of the dozen or so newspaper articles, I knew what my real name was, and where I had lived before the cabin. It was all there, in yellowed black and white, including the name of my sibling.

An article dated approximately a year later carried a photograph of the three of them, sitting in front of a house I didn't recognize. The heading under the picture read, FAMILY OF KIDNAPPED CHILD MAKES NEW

START. *The story told about them moving to a new town, a new house, in an effort to "start over."*

All three of them were smiling.

So they had *cared. They'd been "distraught."*

But they had stopped looking for me. Moved away and made a "new start."

They had loved me once, at least I knew that now. But there was that other child. At some point in their searching, they had decided to give up and devote themselves to the child they still had.

Everything that had happened to me was that child's fault.

I felt like I was on fire with rage, reading those clippings, being reminded of what I had lost, and why I had lost it.

What a wonderful life that other child must have had all these years. A life very like the ones in the books I read. A perfect, happy life with two adoring parents.

The life that should have been mine.

It took me a long time to make my way to where my sibling was. Along the way I learned many, many things about life. Everything was new and foreign to me. Much of the time, I felt like a visitor from another planet. But I kept going. Because I had to. And I kept reading because I knew that I had so much to learn if I didn't want people to keep looking at me in that inquisitive way whenever I did or said the wrong thing.

And finally, finally, just when I was so tired and felt so hopeless that I thought I couldn't go on, I found the town and I found the house.

But I also found that my parents were both dead. That was a bitter pill to swallow, let me tell you. Knowing that after all I'd been through, I would never, ever have the chance to see them again, ask them why they'd stopped looking, ask them why they had moved away to start a new life when for all they knew, I might have come back to that house looking for them one day.

But the sibling wasn't dead. The sibling was very much alive.

And I knew where.

The next day, I was on my way.

"You're bored? You don't like my story. Well, I didn't like it much, either. You don't have anything to do? Here, you can play with this. It's mine, but I don't mind. Just be careful with it, okay? It's very old."

"It's yucky! It's all dirty, and it's stinky."

"You can go into the bathroom and give it a

bath in the sink if you want. Just don't make a mess, okay?"

"Okay."

Yes, I was on my way again. And this time, I didn't plan to stop until I found the person who had been living, all these years, the life I should have been living.

And here I am.

Chapter 18

"It was a false alarm," Reardon told Nora as he and Amy entered the house. He stopped short then, his eyes on her neck. "What happened to your throat, Nora?"

Ignoring the question, she said, her voice heavy with disappointment, "Someone called and lied about where Mindy was? Why would they do that?"

"Well, now that I see those bruises on your neck," Reardon said as Nora led the way down the hall to the kitchen, "I think maybe it had something to do with you. You didn't leave the house, did you? You promised you wouldn't."

"No, I didn't leave the house. Not exactly." Nora was bitterly disappointed by their news. Mindy was still missing? It wasn't over yet?

And if Mindy wasn't safe yet, neither was Nora.

"Not exactly? What does that mean? And what happened to your migraine?" But Reardon didn't seem angry. He must have realized that she'd invented the migraine, and why, and had decided to forgive her for her phony comment about his inability to protect her. He knew now that she hadn't meant it.

"I got lucky. It went away." The only way she was going to find out anything about the cruel hoax played on all of them was to tell them what had happened to her in the back yard. Reardon wouldn't answer any of her questions until she'd answered his.

She told them what had happened, her voice hoarse, one hand gently rubbing her raw throat as she talked.

"I knew I shouldn't have left!" Reardon shouted in exasperation. "And you," to Nora, "you should have known better than to go outside." Then he calmed down. "But that explains the phone call saying Mindy was at the house on Fourth Street."

Nora frowned. "Explains it how?"

"With everyone dispatched to Twin Falls, there'd be no one left to get in his way *here*, right?"

Amy and Nora let that sink in. Then Amy

asked, "You think it was him? The kidnapper? If it was, why didn't he kill her when he had the chance?"

"He isn't ready," Nora answered in a matter-of-fact voice that belied her screaming nerves. "I shouldn't have been able to get away from him this time. He *let* me go. Just gave up when I ran. I thought about that for a while, and the only answer I could come up with was that he's just not ready to finish me off." She looked at both of them with grave eyes. "But I still think he's going to. He's just having fun first."

"Do you have *any* idea why?" Reardon asked, pulling a small notebook from his chest pocket.

Nora shook her head. "No. I don't have a clue."

"A clue," he muttered, replacing the notebook, "that's what we need, a clue. Any clue. There were no fingerprints on the sneaker, none on the box of clippings, the ground's too dry for any footprints, and you didn't recognize the voice you heard."

They sat at the table in glum silence. Outside, the sun had disappeared and the wind had picked up. Nora sensed impending rain in the air.

"There wasn't *any* sign of Mindy at that house?"

Reardon shook his head. "It's abandoned. The neighbors say no one's lived there for over a year. They haven't seen anyone going in or coming out, so Mindy was never there. It was a hoax, that's all. Captain thinks it was a crank, but now that I've heard about the attack on you outside, I'd say it wasn't a crank at all. I'd better go call in."

"You're going to leave us here alone?" Amy cried in alarm, her eyes flying to the back door as if she expected Nora's attacker to be standing there.

"He's just going to the phone, Amy," Nora said, near tears because Mindy hadn't been in Twin Falls and no one had any idea where she might be. "He's not leaving the house."

"How can you be so *calm*?" Amy hissed when Reardon had moved on down the hall toward the telephone. "After what happened to you! When you didn't answer my phone call, I got really nervous. You've been pretty shaky lately. I was afraid you'd done something really stupid, like go to the day care center alone. Going outside alone is almost as bad," she added disapprovingly. "You could have been killed!"

"Why would I go to the day care center?" Nora asked bitterly. "There isn't anything to celebrate, *is* there?"

"No," Amy admitted reluctantly. "But *you* didn't know that."

"Where are Sabra and Fitz? Where's Lucas? Why aren't they with you?"

"The search is still continuing, Nora. No one's giving up. Sabra was going with one team to search all those little rooms at the top of the university tower, and Fitz was headed for the caves on the other side of that old railroad bridge behind campus with another team. Lucas went home. He said he was exhausted." Amy sighed heavily. "Everyone is. I have to go, too, Nora. My team's searching the woods."

The distant rumble of thunder echoed behind the house. This time, Nora was certain, it meant rain. That would make it so much harder to find a little girl in the woods, if that was where Mindy was.

"You'd better get going then," Nora said, although she hated the idea. She wanted Amy to stay. It was comforting, having another girl, a friend, in the house. She hadn't had a good, close friend in a long time. And as long as Amy's car was parked out front, maybe *he* wouldn't come back.

Amy left, saying once again that she'd call the minute she had good news, and Reardon returned. His expression was grim.

"I don't like this," he said apologetically, "but I've been ordered to make sure the house is secure and then station myself in my unit outside to keep an eye on the place. Instead of waiting in here with you."

"You have to leave?" Nora asked, her heart sinking. Amy had gone, and now Reardon was leaving the house?

"Well, I'll be right outside. In front."

"He came around the back of the house this last time," she reminded him. "You won't see him if he does it again. He could come up the hill, through the woods, and through the back door, and you wouldn't even know it."

"It's locked, right?" He moved swiftly to the door to check the lock. "There!" he declared heartily, turning around again. "He can't get in. He'd make so much noise trying to open the door, you'd hear him and come out and get me, right?"

Nora didn't like it, not one bit. Why couldn't he wait in the house with her? She'd feel much safer. "I'll sit in the car with you."

"Nope. Not allowed. Sorry. And the thing is," his eyes avoiding hers, "I think the captain is sort of *hoping* the guy will show up, know what I mean? I think the idea is for me to stop him before he gets inside. And I'll *do* that. You don't have to worry. And catching this guy is the only way this is going to end for you, Nora."

Oh, no, Nora thought instinctively, it's not the *only* way it can end for me. He could slip by you, Reardon, and get to me first. Then it could end in a very different way.

They stood facing each other, feeling the uneasiness between them but each aware that they had no choice.

"Look," he said awkwardly, his eyes on her face, "I'm on duty here, so I need to be careful about what I say and do. But I need to know that *you* know I won't let anything happen to you, okay? You got that?"

She nodded. "Got that." She knew he meant that he didn't *want* anything bad to happen to her. But he suddenly looked so young, so sweet, that she couldn't help adding, "Is your captain sending other officers?"

His face fell.

"All I meant," she amended hastily, "was that this is such a big place for one person to keep any eye on. The house is huge, and then there's the barn and the garage apartment . . ."

"We searched those," he said stiffly. "They're secured."

Nora bristled. This was her *life* she was trying to protect. "They *were* secured. They haven't been checked out in a while. Aren't you supposed to call for back-up or something, like they do on television?"

"That's only when you're ready to apprehend a criminal, Nora. We don't even know that he's still around here."

I know it, Nora thought, her hands so cold with fear, she couldn't feel her fingers. I know he's still here. Somewhere. Waiting to finish me off.

Having Jonah Reardon outside in his car was better than nothing. And he could use his car radio to keep checking every few minutes to see if there was any word on Mindy.

The strained atmosphere between them didn't ease after he had searched the house once more. When he left, all he said was, "I'll be right outside. Lock the door behind me, okay?"

"Jonah . . ."

He turned, his face impassive. "What?"

"I didn't mean," Nora said quietly, "that I didn't trust you to handle things. If it wasn't such a big place . . ."

"Yeah, right." He went out and closed the door.

Nora locked it behind him. She'd have to fix things with him later. This wasn't the time. All she cared about now was having Mindy found before another long, long night passed.

That's not really all you care about, her brain said. You care about staying alive, too.

But she had Reardon, even if he wasn't inside the house. Who did Mindy have to look after her, wherever she was?

Where *was* she?

As if in answer to her question, the phone shrilled.

Nora ran over and picked it up.

"The garage apartment," a voice whispered loudly in her ear. *"And don't bring the cop. If you ever want to see Mindy Donner alive again, sneak out the back way, go through the woods, and come up behind the garage. Do not let him see you. Not if you want him to stay alive. I mean what I say, Nora."*

Click.

Chapter 19

Nora slowly replaced the receiver.

She knew exactly what she should do. She should dash outside to Reardon's car and rap on the window, shout at him to run to the garage apartment and get Mindy.

Maybe Mindy wasn't even there, just as she hadn't been in the house on Fourth Street. But if she *was* in that apartment and her captor saw a policeman getting out of his car and running toward the garage, something terrible could happen to her. Something deadly.

I *have* to go alone, Nora decided, her stomach churning violently. I have to. Maybe Mindy isn't there at all. But if she is, she deserves a chance. She'll have no chance at all if the kidnapper sees a police uniform approaching. And once I'm inside, if she really is there, I'll think of some way to get her out safely.

You're making a terrible mistake, her brain

said as she turned away from the phone. You're not a cop. And there's one right outside. What's the matter with you? Why aren't you calling him?

Because both Reardon *and* Mindy could end up getting killed! Nora shouted silently. Not to mention me. Can't you see that?

You're crazy, her brain replied.

"Right," she muttered, and ran to the back of the house and out the door.

Chapter 20

Mindy Donner's kidnapper stood in the bathroom doorway, leaning casually against the frame, and said, "I want you to stay in here for a while. Since you're busy anyway, that shouldn't be a problem. We're about to have company."

The little girl, her arms covered with suds, her hands diligently scrubbing away with an old, thin, yellow washcloth, looked up with interest. "I like comp'ny. Why can't I come out?" Her lower lip thrust forward. "My daddy lets me see comp'ny. He even lets me stay up late when comp'ny comes."

"I'm not your daddy. You stay here. I'll call you when you can come out."

"You're stinky."

"Yeah, well, things are tough all over, kid. You haven't had it so bad, am I right? Anyway, I'm going to lock the door now. You'll be fine in there. I'll unlock it in a few minutes, I promise. I have to prepare to greet my guest. But first, there's something very important I have to do. Be right back. Don't go away."

The door closed.

"Stinky!" The little girl went back to scrubbing and wasn't distracted by the sound of the door closing.

Nora did as she'd been told. She ran into the back yard and headed straight for the woods.

Something stopped her, just for a second. As she left the porch, the clothesline caught her eye. The animals were gone. All of them. Not a single stuffed, crocheted animal remained.

Nora swallowed hard. It was a message, she knew that. She just didn't know what it meant.

Shaking her head in dismissal, because the missing animals didn't matter now, she cut through the woods behind Nightingale Hall under a sky rapidly darkening from a combination of nightfall and thick, gray clouds.

But it wasn't completely dark yet. She could see, and she knew exactly how to get from the back of the house to the back of the garage with the best chance of not being seen by Reardon.

Once there, though, going up the stairs would be another matter. The staircase was at the side of the garage facing the house. She couldn't be sure if he had a view of those stairs from where he sat. She didn't think so. The car might be parked too far back. She'd just have to hope, and dart up the stairs as quickly as she could.

Her heart was pounding fiercely in her chest, her head throbbing. This is foolish, this is crazy, she told herself as she pushed through a final clump of underbrush and came out of the woods just a few feet from the garage stairs. I should *not* be doing this.

But she kept going. Mindy, she thought frantically, Mindy, are you in there?

Glancing quickly to her left, she was relieved to see no sign of Reardon's car. Nightingale Hall blocked her view of it, and therefore, his view of *her*.

When she reached the foot of the staircase, the house on her right now, she dared another glance toward where the car was parked. If he saw her heading up the stairs . . .

All she could see of the car from her vantage

point was the front license plate and the right front tire.

Breathing a heavy sigh of relief, Nora started up the stairs.

And stopped.

There was something on the narrow, unpainted wooden steps. Small chunks and wedges of something beige in color, rubbery-looking, scattered randomly, like a trail of bread crumbs leading upward.

Nora bent to pick up one of the larger chunks.

And knew immediately what it was.

Shredded foam rubber. Her mother had stuffed the crocheted animals with it. Nora knew that, because holding the rubbery wedge in her hand brought back a sharp memory of when she'd first been given one of the toys. A fat yellow duck, if she remembered correctly. With typical childish curiosity, she had surreptitiously sliced into its round tummy with a nail file to see what was inside that made it so soft. She had been properly scolded and hadn't repeated the act on any subsequent gift.

But she remembered the stuffing material well enough now that she was certain the trail of foam rubber was intended as a message for her.

He had taken the animals from the line and destroyed them? And left the evidence on the steps for her to see?

Why?

Nora hesitated at the foot of the stairs. This is crazy, you can't do this, go back and get Reardon, her brain ordered.

Yes, yes, that was right, that was what she had to do. She'd been foolish to think she could do this by herself. She was not only putting herself in jeopardy, planning to tangle with someone who was clearly dangerous, she could be risking Mindy's life, too.

Reardon was a police officer. He'd know what to do.

Turning away from the littered staircase, Nora had only taken one step forward when a figure appeared from around the corner of the house, just ahead of where Reardon's car was parked, and began hurrying toward her.

Twilight had fallen, and with the dark clouds overhead, Nora had trouble seeing clearly. The figure was tall, like Reardon, swathed in a long, full raincoat, and walked with its head down.

Reardon hadn't been wearing a raincoat. Had he had one in the car?

Nora took another step forward.

"Stay there, Nora!" a voice that wasn't Reardon's called out, waving her back to the staircase. "We have to go up there, to the apartment. Mindy's up there."

Nora knew the voice. It belonged to Sabra Nicks. And a moment later, she saw that it was indeed Sabra's face above the collar of the yellow raincoat. Her dark hair blew in the wind as she hurried toward Nora. "Mindy? Up there? Are you serious?"

Sabra nodded. She reached Nora's side. But the expression on her face wasn't one of complete joy. "Yes, that's what I came to tell you. But you're not going to like it, Nora. I know how much you liked him."

"Sabra, Mindy can't be up there," Nora argued, wishing that were so, but failing to see how it could be. "The police searched that apartment. There wasn't anyone there."

"That's because he hid in the woods. With Mindy. He saw the police at Nightmare Hall and he put Mindy in a laundry bag, tossed her over his shoulder, and walked right out of the apartment. No one saw him, but even if they had, they would have thought you were letting him do his laundry at the house. Because he's a friend of yours, Nora. Someone you trust.

But he's confessed. He told the police everything."

"Who?" Nora breathed. She had so few friends. "Who took Mindy?"

"Fitz."

"No . . ."

"He did, Nora. I don't know the whole story yet, only what Reardon told me a few minutes ago, but it's got something to do with Fitz's sister dying when he was little. Remember, he told us? Mindy reminded him of the pictures of his sister, and I guess it sent him off the deep end. He never helped with the search, Nora. He just went and signed up and then left, came back here. There were so many people searching, he wasn't missed. Anyway," Sabra turned to glance up the stairs, "he told the police that Mindy is here, in this apartment. So, what are we waiting for? Let's go get her. Man, is she going to be happy to see us!"

"Why isn't Reardon coming with us?" Nora asked, trying to take in what Sabra had told her.

"He is. But he was on the radio to headquarters when I left. He'll be right along. Come on, how can you stand to wait another second? Fitz is in jail, Nora, it's all over. There's nothing to be afraid of now. No more nasty phone calls, no more ropes around your neck . . ."

Nora jerked backward, against the wall of the garage. Her spine tingling, she stared at Sabra. Fitz wouldn't have, she thought, he wouldn't have. And Sabra hadn't been with Reardon and Amy when they came back to Nightingale Hall and saw the bruises on her neck. How did she *know* about the rope?

Fitz wouldn't have. He adored Mindy.

"I think," Nora said lightly, willing her voice not to shake, "that I'll just go get Reardon, okay? We should have a cop with us when we go up there, really." She took a step forward, would have made an end run around Sabra then, but the taller girl's eyes narrowed and she moved to block Nora's exit.

"Oh, no, I don't think so," she said smoothly. "You're not going anywhere except upstairs, to that apartment. Mindy really is up there, Nora, I promise. She's been there the whole time, except for once or twice when we were forced to leave temporarily." Her eyes were cold and hard now, filled with hatred, her smile thin and angry.

She reached out, took Nora's elbow in what proved to be a painfully firm grip, and said, "Now walk! Up the stairs, like a good girl. I'll be right behind you, little sister, so if you stumble and fall, I can catch you. Isn't that what big sisters are for?"

She began pushing Nora up the stairs to the apartment.

Chapter 21

"And don't worry about that cute cop who's been hanging around you," Sabra added, her fingers tightening on Nora's elbow. "I took care of him. The police can be such an awful nuisance, can't they?"

Speechless with confusion created by the hateful look on Sabra's face and the things she was saying, Nora tried to pull away from the ironlike grip. In vain. The fingers maintained their grip.

"You wanted to see Mindy? You shall see Mindy. Right this way, Madam," Sabra said in an affected voice. "Please accompany me to my temporary residence." And she whipped a key from her raincoat pocket and opened the apartment door, shoving Nora inside before turning to close and lock the door again. She slid the key into a jeans pocket and moved out into the middle of the room, and began pulling Nora up the staircase.

"Sabra, what's going on?" Nora asked, staying near the door, her back to it. She glanced anxiously around the one-room apartment. "Where is Mindy? And why isn't Reardon here yet?"

Sabra smirked. "Supposed to be watching out for you, is he? Then he shouldn't be so friendly to people he *thinks* are friends of yours. Rolled that window down easy as pie, he did, when I tapped on the window. Even smiled at me. He really is cute, sister dear. I wouldn't let that one get away if I were you." They were at the top of the stairs. Sabra giggled. "Oh, sorry, I forgot. Silly me. You're not going to be around to pursue a relationship with anyone, little sister."

"Sabra, what are you doing?" For one confused second, Nora wondered if Sabra thought of them as being in a "sisterhood" of some kind, as if they were members of the same sorority. "Why do you keep calling me that?"

"She *is* here, you know," Sabra said, walking over to the far side of the room, turning to lean against a squat, black cookstove. "Mindy. She's been here the whole time."

"With you? Not Fitz? You?"

"I never hurt her, Nora. I took good care of her."

Nora struggled to understand what was going on. Sabra had taken Mindy? Had had her all this time? "When you were telling me what Fitz did . . . you were talking about *you*?"

"Yep." Sabra's expression changed to one of smugness. "I knew you wouldn't buy that story about Fitz. You like him too much. But it was worth a shot."

"Mindy?" Nora called then, glancing around the large, blue-walled room. "Mindy, are you here?" A sofabed, extended fully and made up with rumpled sheets and a blanket, stood against one wall. There was a recliner next to it facing a television set in a squat, dark cabinet, a blue wooden table and two chairs in the kitchen area and other, smaller pieces of furniture scattered about the area. But there was no sign of a little girl with curly hair.

"Norrie? Norrie, this door is locked!"

Nora gasped, her gaze flying to the only door in the room, off to her left. "Mindy, is that you?"

"Norrie, let me out. Saber won't let me. You do it, Norrie."

Nora lunged forward, but Sabra shouted,

"Stay where you are! In fact, take a seat. We'll be here a while."

Nora sat, worried about Mindy's safety if Sabra became too angry.

"She can stay in there a little while longer. It won't kill her. Besides, you don't owe her anything, Nora." A sly smile crossed her face. "It's not like you're related to her. Not like you are to me, sister dearest."

"Just a minute, honey," Nora called to Mindy. "I'll get you out, I promise." To Sabra, she said, "That's the third time you've called me that. Your sister." Nora glanced at the bathroom door. The key to it was probably on Sabra's person somewhere. "We're not sisters."

"Oh, but we are." Contempt filled Sabra's face. "Oh, jeez, Nora, you're not going to play the innocent on me, are you? That would just be too disgusting."

"I don't know what you're talking about. I'm an only child, Sabra. And you said you came from a really big family. I don't come from a really big family. How could we be sisters?"

"Oh, for crying out loud, I made up that stupid story. I even added a father who drank so that my family life wouldn't sound too perfect to be true. I couldn't tell the truth about the way I'd been raised. Everyone would have thought I was *really* weird. Because it *was* weird, Nora. Not like the way you were raised, in a nice, big house with two loving, happy parents. And I should have been there, too. I belonged there." Sabra lifted her head. "My real name, something I just learned recently, is Nell Mulgrew. And I *am* your sister, older by two years. I was kidnapped when I was five and you were three."

Nora stared at her, her mouth agape. "That's crazy! I'd know if I'd had a sister! I would *know* that, Sabra!"

"You *do* know it!" Sabra shouted, "You do! You have to. Quit pretending, Nora. You're not a very good actress."

"I'm not acting, Sabra. I never had an older sister. Never!" But even as she said it, little bits and pieces of images began to swirl around in Nora's brain . . . none of them complete, none of them as vivid as her other, recent memories. She heard a distant, unfamiliar voice, the voice of a child, calling her name, saw herself playing in the bathtub along with the shadowy figure of another child, felt the softness of a pillow whacking her in the head and saw a pair of thin arms opposite her reaching up to throw another pillow. All of it was vague, shadowy, and oddly painful.

"No," Nora whispered, "no, I'd remember . . ."

"I'll prove it to you," Sabra said hotly. She strode over to the bathroom door, pulled a key from her pocket, and unlocked the door.

Mindy stood behind it, her hair tousled, her chin dotted with suds. She was holding something fat and brown and so heavy with water that she was having trouble handling it.

Sabra snatched the wet thing from Mindy's arms as the child ran to Nora, and held it up. "Do you see this?" she shouted at Nora. "Do you?"

Nora folded Mindy into her arms, then pulled her up on her lap. "What is it? It's so wet, I can't tell what it is."

Sabra thrust it under her nose. "It's Barney the bear. Don't you recognize it? Mama gave it to me, the same time she gave you Harry the hippo. I wanted to trade, because I liked Harry better, but you wouldn't. Selfish. You were always selfish."

Nora stared at the thing Sabra was holding in front of her. When she saw the stitching, the crocheted loops, the dark brown fake glass eyes, she realized what she was looking at. Her mind spun, her senses reeled. Barney the bear? Barney the *bear*?

"Trade with me, Norrie, I'm the oldest, I should get my pick, and I like Harry the hippo the best. Come on, Norrie, don't be stingy!" The smaller girl clung stubbornly to the fat, gray hippo. The older girl, tall and spindly, with dark hair unlike the mother's and the other child's fair, wispy hair, said angrily, *"Oh, Norrie, you are the most spoildest sister anyone ever had. I hate you!"*

Nora gasped and clung to Mindy. "I . . . I don't . . ."

Sabra ran to the kitchen counter and snatched up a sheaf of yellowed newspapers. Brought them back to Nora, shoved them at her. "Here, read! Read, and then tell me I'm not Nell Mulgrew."

Feeling dizzy, as if the words Sabra had spoken were hammers that had been striking at her skull, Nora read.

When she had finished, her face was completely drained of color. The clippings in her hand shook violently as she tried to regain control of her thoughts and her emotions. But the words she had read had triggered an onslaught of scraps and bits of memory long forgotten.

A girl, wearing a bright red jacket and red rubber boots, playing in the snow behind a huge, white house, laughing, throwing snowballs, teasing, "Norrie, Norrie, you don't know how to throw at all. Mommy should teach you."

The same girl, standing at the top of the slide on a summer day yellow and hot with sunshine, calling, "You can't climb up that way, Norrie, Mommy don't let us."

Another day, cold and rainy, sitting on a window seat in the living room while someone read a children's book in a soft, sweet voice, and an arm not much larger than Nora's was around her shoulders, warm and friendly. Not her mother's arm, too small. And a voice saying, "We didn't like that story, did we, Norrie? You better read us another one, Mommy, one we like better."

Her mother crying out, "Nell, oh, Nell, I miss you so!"

Nell. Not the grandmother named Nell. The child named Nell.

Nora leaned back in the chair, her head resting against the worn upholstery. "I can't believe I forgot," she whispered, tears filling her eyes. "How could I have forgotten? I remember now, everyone was crying all the time and then they went on television and begged to get their little girl back and it didn't work, she didn't come back, and Mama never stopped crying and then she got sick . . ."

"Do you remember the woman coming out of the woods that winter day when I was only five years old?" Sabra asked harshly. "Do you remember that you didn't lift a finger to help me as she snatched me up and carried me away? Do you remember that you didn't call for help or run to get our mother?"

Nora stared at her. "Sabra . . . you said you were older than me by two years. If you were five years old when you were kidnapped, then I was only three. Three, Sabra! What could I have done? I probably didn't even know what was happening."

It came back then, one more memory, painfully vivid, of her distraught mother shouting at her, "Why didn't you *do* something?"

Which, she realized now, was why she had thought forever after that her mother's bouts with illness were her fault. And blaming herself *had* started very young. She'd simply forgotten that, as she'd forgotten so many things. To protect herself, maybe. Wasn't that usually why people forgot bad things?

She could think of nothing more to say. What was there to say?

She was looking at her own sister, and the eyes that looked back at her were filled with hate and anger.

"Is that why you hate me?" Nora asked then. "Because you think I should have stopped it somehow? Even though I was only three?"

Sabra threw the bear, heavy with water, at her in disgust. The blow hurt. "That's not why!" she shouted, brushing a lock of dark hair away from her face. "It's because you had everything I never had, everything I was supposed to have. A nice house, a wonderful life, two loving parents, a happy home . . ."

Nora laughed. It was just a small laugh, bitter and harsh, at first. But any control she had had over her emotions had been destroyed by the incredible news that Sabra had presented her with, and the small laugh escalated into peal after peal of high, shrill, humorless laughter, and as Mindy looked up at her in concern and Sabra stared at her, Nora threw her head back and laughed and laughed until tears spilled down her cheeks, burning like acid.

Chapter 22

It was the horrified look on Mindy's face that snapped Nora back to reality and interrupted her hysteria in mid-laugh.

Swiping at her eyes, she hugged the child and gasped, "It's okay, honey. I'm okay. I just thought something that Sabra said was really funny, that's all." To Sabra, she said, "Why did you do all of this? Why did you take Mindy? And try to hurt me? What does all of this have to do with what happened then?"

Sabra had backed away, returned to lean against the stove, and was staring at Nora with uneasy eyes. "You are acting really weird. What was all that crazy laughing about?"

In a weary voice, Nora told her. Explained that Sabra had been wrong, so very wrong. Told her that after the kidnapping, nothing was ever the same. Her mother had been ill repeatedly. They had moved, more than once.

No more big, white house with the pony in the back yard, rabbits in the pen, no gardens, no familiar faces, everything different. From that day on, the life they had known when they were little disappeared completely. Then the parents' deaths, so close together, the unfriendly aunt taking an orphan into the cramped, dreary apartment, the stay in the hospital, the loss of memory. "It wasn't what you thought it was at all," Nora finished without emotion. "Not even close."

There was a stunned, blank look on Sabra's face.

"Are you okay, honey?" Nora asked Mindy, who sat in her lap, humming contentedly, not even nagging about when her daddy was coming to get her. "You're not hurt, are you?"

"She's not hurt!" Sabra said sharply, snapping out of her shock. "I took good care of her." Then, "I suppose you think that sob story you just told me makes a difference, don't you? Not that I believe a word of it."

"I can prove it," Nora replied defiantly. "Go to the phone right now and call my Aunt Colleen. I'll be happy to give you her number. And yes, I do think it makes a difference. You hate me because all this time you thought I had such a wonderful life. Well, I didn't. It wasn't horrible, but it wasn't the way you pictured it. So yes, it should make a difference."

"The woman is *my* aunt, too," Sabra said angrily, clearly flustered by the drastic alteration in the fantasy she had bitterly nurtured for so long. "Don't forget that. You said '*my*' Aunt Colleen, as if she was your private, personal property."

"Sorry. Is that why you did all of this? Kidnapping Mindy, trying to remind me of your kidnapping, is that what you were doing? And then trying to hurt me, just to make me suffer the way you did? Was that it? And planting those things of Mindy's in my room. You were planning to frame me, weren't you? You did all of that because you thought I lived such a wonderful life?"

"Don't you think it's appropriate? A kidnapping ruined *my* life. I wanted this one to ruin yours."

"How?"

"Well, for one thing, I knew you'd *care*. I knew how attached you were to Mindy, so her kidnapping would certainly hurt you as much as it would anyone except her parents. And second, yes, I *did* want to remind you. All those years, I just assumed you remembered. And that you'd just put it out of your mind and gone on with your life as if it hadn't happened. That made me really mad. That day we all talked about our families, you never mentioned having a sister who had been kidnapped. That made me so furious! As if it had never happened."

"I didn't know that it had," Nora reminded her.

Disgust flooded Sabra's face. "How could you forget something so horrible? I was more determined than ever after that day. And yes, I *was* planning on making it look like you'd done it. It hasn't worked so far, or you'd have been arrested by now, but it still could. I could say I found you here with Mindy, we struggled, and I had to kill you to save her."

Sabra said the words so matter-of-factly that Nora almost failed to grasp the meaning. When she did, an involuntary gasp escaped her lips. "That would never work," she protested weakly. "Mindy would tell. She'd tell them I hadn't kidnapped her."

"Well, yeah, I get that now. I'd have to make a few minor changes, that's all. I thought she'd be as useless as you were when you were three, but she isn't. I know she could hang me. She's very bright. But I could always make more adjustments."

Nora's heart turned over. "Like?"

"Like, the new plan could be, I don't show up until you've already eighty-sixed the kid, maybe with a pillow over her face. Then I find you out, go for the phone to call the cops, you attack me, etcetera, etcetera." Sabra smiled slyly. "In case you haven't noticed, we are now more than halfway through that scenario. Just a few more loose ends to tie up, and that won't take long."

When Nora didn't say anything because her mind was racing, struggling to figure out a way to circumvent Sabra's plan, Sabra added, "But it would never work. I would love to see you in prison for the rest of your life. The way I was in prison. But that's not going to happen. The police aren't going to buy a frame, or they'd have arrested you by now. Anyway, your little cop friend, Reardon, certainly wouldn't buy it."

Nora felt a rush of warmth that helped, just a little, against the full body chill she was feeling, listening to Sabra. "No, Reardon wouldn't buy it."

"There are other solutions." Sabra thought for a minute, then said calmly, "You'll just have to die, that's all. There's no way around that." Thought for another minute or two, ignoring Nora's gasp of horror, before adding, "I didn't know you'd been in the hospital. That's definitely a bonus. People wouldn't have any trouble believing you went off the deep end. They're already very suspicious of you." She fixed dark, empty eyes on the ceiling. "But never mind. I don't care anymore what they think when they find us. It won't matter then."

Nora clutched Mindy harder. "When they find us?"

And then, still staring blankly at the ceiling, Sabra told Nora, in a flat, unemotional voice, the same story she had shared with Mindy over the long hours in the apartment. Mindy hadn't understood it.

But Nora did.

"I'm . . . sorry," was all she could manage when Sabra had finished talking and fallen morbidly silent. "I'm really sorry. It sounds horrible. But I can't believe you blame me. A three-year-old?"

"If they hadn't had you," Sabra said, turning toward the stove, "they would have kept looking for me." Then she reached over to turn on all four gas burners.

Alarmed, Nora sat up straight up in her chair, nearly spilling Mindy to the floor. The soaking-wet bear, still in Nora's lap, suddenly seemed to weigh a ton and she was vaguely aware of a large, uncomfortable, wet spot on her shorts. "What are you doing?"

Gas began to hiss from the jets.

"You need a match to light the burners on this stove," Sabra said, smiling vaguely. "Trouble is, I just don't happen to have any matches. Sorry about that."

The apartment was not that large. The unmistakable odor of gas was already perceptible.

Sabra reached into her pocket and pulled out a match. "Well, whatya know?" she said, still smiling. "I found one, after all."

Terrified, beginning to shake, Nora said, "You'll kill us all!"

The match still unlit in her hand, Sabra turned and her smile now was different. Not the least bit vague or dreamy-eyed. This was a cold, empty smile, without feeling, and her eyes held the same emptiness. "I died a long time ago. At least, Nell Mulgrew did. It's Sabra Nicks who will go up in flames, and Sabra Nicks has no life. Won't have a life, ever. Did you know I'm not really a student here? Never could be. I never went to school, did I tell you that? Yeah, I guess I did. I wanted to, but . . . I just pretended to be a student here. No one ever checked, although I suppose they would have once the fall semester started. I'm smart enough, from reading. But I don't even have a high school diploma."

Although her voice still held no emotion of any kind, Nora, sitting on the edge of her chair, her body tensed and frozen, thought she saw a glittering in Sabra's eyes that could easily have been the beginning of tears.

"Sabra . . . Nell . . ." Nora tried, "you can't do this. You cannot do this. I'll help you do whatever you want with your life, I promise. Anything I can. I didn't forget you on purpose, it was the medication, at least partly. Please, please, think of Mindy. None of this is her fault. Please, Sabra. You can have a life now, if you want it. You *can!*"

The big, stuffed bear, saturated with water, suddenly shifted position, slid heavily down Nora's thighs and came to rest on her knees. But she never took her eyes off the girl standing at the stove, match in hand.

This can't happen, Nora told herself, her body so tense her joints ached. This cannot be allowed to happen. Not to Mindy. Not to me. Not even to Sabra . . . Nell. She hadn't killed anyone. She didn't deserve to die. None of them did.

This could not be allowed to happen.

The door was useless. The key was in Sabra's pocket. Nora tried to judge the distance between her chair and the stove. Impossible. She'd never make it in time.

She glanced wildly about the room, her eyes frantic. Something to throw, something to use as a weapon . . .

The bear pressed down hard on her knees.

"It's too late," Sabra announced calmly. "I can't have anything now. Not ever." And she turned back to the stove, extending her arm to strike the match against it.

Nora snatched up the waterlogged bear, jumped to her feet and, taking just one tiny fraction of a second to steady her arm and aim, flung the toy at Sabra.

It caught her on the side of the head, just above the temple, and sent her sailing away from the stove and into the wall. Her head hit hard, leaving a dent in the wallboard. Her knees buckled. She remained upright for just another second or two, a look of acceptance on her face, as if she wasn't at all surprised to find that even this last desperate plan had failed. Then her eyes closed and she slid to the floor.

Nora rushed to the stove to turn off the jets. She stooped to yank the door key out of Sabra's jeans pocket, then ran back to a bewildered

Mindy, scooped her up, and ran to the door to unlock it and fling it open.

The fresh air felt wonderful.

But there was no time to rejoice. Sabra was still inside, the gas stove was still there, she still had the match, and thought she had no reason to live. If she came to . . .

Mindy in her arms, Nora staggered down the wooden staircase and stumbled to Reardon's car. The window was still down, the way Sabra had left it and for one terrible moment, when she saw him sitting limply behind the wheel, his head tilted to one side, she thought he was dead.

But when she called to him, reached in through the window to shake his shoulder, he murmured and began coming around.

"Jonah, wake up!" she shouted, setting Mindy down on the ground, telling her not to move one step. "You have to use your radio to call for help. Get an ambulance. Hurry! Jonah, wake *up!*"

He came around, gingerly rubbing the lump on the back of his head. "A rock!" he mumbled. "She hit me with a rock!"

Becoming aware of his surroundings, he glanced anxiously at Nora. "You okay? You're not hurt? I feel like such an idiot, trusting that girl." Then he spotted Mindy and his expression brightened. "That's her? You found her?"

"Never mind that now," Nora said frantically, "you've got to call for help. She could blow up the whole garage if we don't hurry."

He did as she asked, and that done, joined her on her race back to the garage.

They were almost there when a figure, one hand to its head, staggered through the door.

"Oh, God, that's her," Nora whispered as she and Reardon stopped in their tracks, looking up.

"I guess she changed her mind," Reardon said. "If she was going to blow up the place, she'd have done it by now."

The figure moved to the railing surrounding the small platform at the top of the steep staircase.

"Sabra?" Nora called. "Nell?"

Sabra looked down. And although Nora couldn't see her face through the darkness, she could feel the expression of hopelessness there.

"I forgot you, too," the voice said with just a hint of defiance. "I would never have remembered you if it hadn't been for the newspaper clippings."

It sounded like a lie.

Then Sabra climbed up on the railing and

without a moment of hesitation, jumped, her long, yellow raincoat flying out around her like a cape.

It wasn't her scream of terror that filled the humid night air.

It was Nora's.

Epilogue

The promised rain had finally arrived, falling lightly and gently.

Nora sat on the bottom step of the garage staircase, Reardon's light blue jacket around her shoulders, her hair damp with raindrops, watching as the ambulance attendants loaded the unconscious Sabra onto a stretcher.

"I'm glad she's not dead." Nora's voice was soft. She didn't want Mindy, sitting happily in the front seat of a nearby police car waiting for the arrival of her father, to hear what she was saying. The child seemed unharmed by her ordeal, and Nora didn't want to upset her. Not that Mindy seemed at all upset. Annoyed, remarking when the policemen arrived on the scene that her daddy hadn't picked a very good "baby-sitter" for her this time. But not upset or frightened. That was a big relief.

So maybe hearing the conversation about Sa-bra . . . *Nell* . . . wouldn't have upset her. Still, Nora kept her voice low. "I know she did some terrible things, really terrible. But from what I know so far, she's had an awful life. Wouldn't what she went through make anyone crazy? I don't blame her for hating me, either. All that time, she thought my life was so very different from what it really was." She fell silent, then added with awe in her voice, "I still can't believe I forgot I had a sister. How could I forget that? How could anyone?"

"You were only three, Nora," Jonah reminded her. "Most people don't remember anything that happened before they were five. Not consciously, anyway. And you said your parents never, ever mentioned her, right?"

Nora nodded. "I suppose my father was afraid it would set my mother off again, talking about Nell. There were no pictures, no scrapbooks, no nothing. No sign of her anywhere in the house. That is just so weird."

"Maybe not. If she'd died, they probably would have kept memorabilia of her around the house. But the way she was taken, and the fact that they searched and searched and then finally gave up, was probably so depressing that they couldn't bear to be reminded of it."

Nora looked at him with a steady gaze. "That makes them cowards, doesn't it?"

He shrugged. "In a way, I guess. But some people just can't face reality, especially an ugly reality. That doesn't make them bad people." He shook his head. "Speaking of forgetting things, I just remembered tonight where I'd seen that stuffed bear. But you already know, right? It was in Sabra's car. I had to give her a speeding ticket in town a couple of weeks ago, and the bear was sitting on the front seat. But I completely forgot that was where I'd seen it. Until tonight. Until it was too late."

"Even if you'd remembered," Nora pointed out gently, "you would never have connected that bear or Sabra with Mindy's kidnapping. Why would you? You'd have thought it was just a coincidence that she had an animal like the ones I gave Mindy, right?"

Amy and Fitz, who had been sitting upstairs in the apartment talking to the policemen, came outside and joined Nora and Reardon on the stairs.

"I bought her story about being from a

big family," Amy said bitterly. "She made it sound so real. And I was jealous, I remember that. Growing up an only child, like Lucas, only not liking it as much as he did, I remember wishing I'd had lots of brothers and sisters, like Sabra . . . Nell, I mean. But," she added quickly, "I wouldn't want a sister like her. Doesn't that scare you, Nora? Having someone like that in your family? She's very unstable . . ."

"So was my mother," Nora answered quietly, lifting her rain-streaked face to Amy, who sat one step above her. "But now I know why, and I understand. I thought she was just crazy, and I was always afraid I'd be like her, especially after I went into the hospital when I was fifteen. That scared me half to death. But now I know that what my mother really suffered from was intense grief. Grief over a missing child, with no closure for her loss. She never knew what happened to my sister, and that not knowing affected her mind. I think it would any mother's. That kind of grief isn't inherited. So now I know I'll be okay."

"Then what happened to your sister?" Fitz asked. "Why did she go off the deep end like that?"

Nora sighed. "She couldn't help it. I think she'll get better. With the right kind of care, I think after a while, maybe a long while, she'll be okay. And if she is, then I'll have a family again. Just a little one, but a family." She stood up and took Jonah Reardon's hand, not caring in the least if his fellow officers saw. If she had her way, they'd be seeing a lot of her from now on. "But I'm not going to tell you why she did it out here, in the rain. Take me to Vinnie's and feed me, and I'll tell you my sister's story. It's not pretty, but you all knew Sabra, and I think you should all know why she did what she did. And then maybe," leaving the stairs, walking toward Reardon's police car, her hand still in his, "maybe someday you can know Nell, too. Like I plan to."

A car came racing up the driveway, screeched to a halt on the gravel, and Professor Donner jumped out and rushed to scoop his daughter out of the police car and hold her tightly against his chest.

"Look, Norrie!" the child cried as Nora opened the door to Reardon's car. "My daddy's here!"

Professor Donner sent Nora a heartfelt look of apology over the top of his daughter's curly head.

"I see that he is, sweetie. I told you he would come, didn't I?"

"Yeah, and I knew you weren't fibbing, Norrie."

Nora was still holding the sodden bear in her hands. "Norrie?" Mindy asked. "Can I have the bear? I really, really like him. And I gived him a bath."

Nora hesitated, her hand on the door of Reardon's car. Mindy had been through a lot. An old stuffed, crocheted bear didn't seem like much to ask in return for being taken from her family and held captive, no matter how kind Sabra had been to her.

But . . . Sabra . . . Nell had been through a lot, too. Much worse than what Mindy had gone through. For many years. And no daddy had ever come to get her and take her home.

Nora clutched the bear to her chest. "Gee, honey, I'm sorry," she said, smiling at Mindy, "but I'll have to find another animal in my trunk for you. I think there's an ostrich in there somewhere. With pink wings. Very pretty. I'm afraid the bear belongs to someone else. It belongs to . . . my sister. And she really, really needs it. Okay?"

"What's an ostrik?" Mindy asked, settling back into her father's arms.

About the Author

"Writing tales of horror makes it hard to convince people that I'm a nice, gentle person," says **Diane Hoh**.

"So what's a nice woman like me doing scaring people?

"Discovering the fearful side of life: what makes the heart pound, the adrenalin flow, the breath catch in the throat. And hoping always that the reader is having a frightfully good time, too."

Diane Hoh grew up in Warren, Pennsylvania. Since then, she has lived in New York, Colorado, and North Carolina, before settling in Austin, Texas. "Reading and writing take up most of my life," says Hoh, "along with family, music, and gardening." Her other horror novels include *Funhouse*, *The Accident*, *The Invitation*, *The Fever*, and *The Train*.

Return to Nightmare Hall
if you dare . . .

The Dummy

Betrayal. It's always out there, lapping at my heels like a vicious dog. Just when you think you're finally on safe ground, betrayal sneaks up behind you and rips the ground right out from underneath you, leaving you feeling dizzy and sick and off balance.

Well, not this time. This time, I'm going to have what I've always wanted, no matter what it takes.

I mean that. No matter what it takes.

I would kill to have what I want.

I may have to.

I will not be betrayed again.

THRILLERS

D.E. Athkins
- ☐ MC45246-0 Mirror, Mirror — $3.25
- ☐ MC45349-1 The Ripper — $3.25

A. Bates
- ☐ MC45829-9 The Dead Game — $3.25
- ☐ MC43291-5 Final Exam — $3.25
- ☐ MC44582-0 Mother's Helper — $3.25
- ☐ MC44238-4 Party Line — $3.25

Caroline B. Cooney
- ☐ MC44316-X The Cheerleader — $3.25
- ☐ MC41641-3 The Fire — $3.25
- ☐ MC43806-9 The Fog — $3.25
- ☐ MC45681-4 Freeze Tag — $3.25
- ☐ MC45402-1 The Perfume — $3.25
- ☐ MC44884-6 The Return of the Vampire — $2.95
- ☐ MC41640-5 The Snow — $3.99
- ☐ MC45680-6 The Stranger — $3.50
- ☐ MC45682-2 The Vampire's Promise — $3.50

Richie Tankersley Cusick
- ☐ MC43115-3 April Fools — $3.25
- ☐ MC43203-6 The Lifeguard — $3.25
- ☐ MC43114-5 Teacher's Pet — $3.25
- ☐ MC44235-X Trick or Treat — $3.50

Carol Ellis
- ☐ MC46411-6 Camp Fear — $3.25
- ☐ MC44768-8 My Secret Admirer — $3.25
- ☐ MC47101-5 Silent Witness — $3.25
- ☐ MC46044-7 The Stepdaughter — $3.25
- ☐ MC44916-8 The Window — $3.25

Lael Littke
- ☐ MC44237-6 Prom Dress — $3.50

Jane McFann
- ☐ MC46690-9 Be Mine — $3.25

Christopher Pike
- ☐ MC43014-9 Slumber Party — $3.50
- ☐ MC44256-2 Weekend — $3.50

Edited by T. Pines
- ☐ MC45256-8 Thirteen — $3.99

Sinclair Smith
- ☐ MC45063-8 The Waitress — $3.50

Barbara Steiner
- ☐ MC46425-6 The Phantom — $3.50

Robert Westall
- ☐ MC41693-6 Ghost Abbey — $3.25
- ☐ MC43761-5 The Promise — $3.25
- ☐ MC45176-6 Yaxley's Cat — $3.25

Available wherever you buy books, or use this order form.

Scholastic Inc., P.O. Box 7502, 2931 East McCarty Street, Jefferson City, MO 65102

Please send me the books I have checked above. I am enclosing $_____ (please add $2.00 to cover shipping and handling). Send check or money order — no cash or C.O.D.s please.

Name_____ Age _____

Address_____

City_____ State/Zip_____

Please allow four to six weeks for delivery. Offer good in the U.S. only. Sorry, mail orders are not available to residents of Canada. Prices subject to change.

T295